# AN INTERVIEW WITH MICHAEL MARTONE
## BY MATT BAKER

# AN INTERVIEW WITH MICHAEL MARTONE BY MATT BAKER

*A Product of The Collective*
*2015*

Durham, North Carolina

An Interview with Michael Martone
Copyright ©2025 by Matt Baker and Matthew Baker

This work is licensed under a CC0 License through Creative Commons; this means the authors of the work have waived all of their rights to the work; you can copy, modify, distribute, and perform the work, even for commercial purposes, all without asking permission. Names, characters, business, events and incidents are the products of the author's imagination. Any resemblance to actual persons, living or dead, or actual events is purely coincidental.

Library of Congress Cataloging-in-Publication Data

Names: Baker, Matt, 1984 November 5- author.
Title: An interview with Michael Martone / by Matt Baker.
Identifiers: LCCN 2024036227 (print) | LCCN 2024036228 (ebook) | ISBN 9781949344455 (paperback) | ISBN 9781949344462 (ebook)
Subjects: LCSH: Martone, Michael--Fiction. | LCGFT: Biographical fiction.
Classification: LCC PS3602.A5866345 I58 2025 (print) | LCC PS3602.A5866345 (ebook) | DDC 813/.6--dc23/eng/20240816
LC record available at https://lccn.loc.gov/2024036227
LC ebook record available at https://lccn.loc.gov/2024036228

Published in the United States of America
Cover design by Savannah Bradley
Book design by Spock and Associates

Published by
BULL CITY PRESS
1217 Odyssey Drive
Durham, NC 27713
www.BullCityPress.com

# ACKNOWLEDGMENTS

"An Interview with Michael Martone" originally appeared in *Meridian*; "An Interview with Michael Martone" originally appeared in *Versal*; "An Interview with Michael Martone" originally appeared in *Ninth Letter*; "An Interview with Michael Martone" originally appeared in *Devil's Lake*; "An Interview with Michael Martone" originally appeared in *HTMLGIANT*; "An Interview with Michael Martone" originally appeared in *Pank*; excerpts from "An Interview with Michael Martone" originally appeared in *Hayden's Ferry Review*, *Redivider*, and *Booth*; "An Interview with Michael Martone" originally appeared in *Southern Indiana Review*; "An Interview with Michael Martone" originally appeared in *Hobart*.

# AN INTERVIEW WITH MICHAEL MARTONE BY MATT BAKER

*More imposter than scholar,
more burglar than scribe,
a child born in a fortress among flat lands:
then every border shall burn.*
Nostradamus, "Century XVI," *The Prophecies*

# PREFACE

What follows are nine interviews, eight of which are fictional. All nine interviews were published as nonfiction. All nine interviews were written between 2007–2011 and published between 2009–2013.

Each interview, including the nonfictional, includes previously unpublished material.

Those interested in suing the authors should contact Paul French.

# AN INTERVIEW WITH MICHAEL MARTONE

Depending on whom you ask, Michael Martone is either contemporary literature's most notorious prankster, innovator, or mutineer. In 1985 his AAP membership was briefly revoked after Martone published his first two books—a "prose" collection titled *Alive and Dead in Indiana* and a "poetry" collection titled *Seeing Eye*—which, aside from *Seeing Eye*'s line breaks, were word-for-word identical. His membership to the League of Canadian Writers was revoked in 1999 after LCW discovered that, while Martone's registered nom de plume had been "born" in the hamlet of Titanic, Martone himself never even had been to Canada. His AWP membership was revoked in 2007, reinstated in 2008, and revoked again in 2010.

After his first two books, Martone went on to write *Michael Martone*, a collection of fictional contributor's notes originally published among nonfictional contributor's notes in cooperative journals; *The Blue Guide to Indiana*, a collection of travel articles reviewing fictional attractions such as the Field of Lightbulbs and the memorial to the Muncie Corn Embargo of 1954 (most of which were, again, originally published as nonfiction); fictional interviews with his mentor John Barth; fictional advertisements in the margins of magazines such as *Harper's* and *The Southern Review*; poems using the names of nonfictional colleagues; and blurbs for nonexistent books.

But his latest book is perhaps the most revealing: *Racing in Place* is a collection of essays exploring his obsession with subways, blimps, and cattle, symbols of "this contradiction, this static motion in the Midwest." Born in Fort Wayne, Indiana, Martone is often described as a regionalist, and his relationship with the Midwest mirrors his relationship with literature: he thinks of the Midwest as a "strange, imaginary place" with no distinct borders or boundaries.

Although Martone now teaches at the University of Alabama, he has also taught at Syracuse, Harvard, Brown, and CUNY. Visiting former colleagues in

Manhattan, Martone arranges to meet me near the Williamsburg Bridge for our interview, which he insists be conducted on the subway. "I'll be the one who looks like David Byrne, but younger, and less emaciated," he says. This, too, turns out to lie somewhere between fiction and nonfiction: when I meet him, he looks almost nothing like Byrne, but still more like Byrne than anyone else.

This interview was conducted on the J train in New York City, between the hours of 9 p.m. and 1 a.m.

■ ■ ■
■ ■ ■
■ ■ ■

*I've read that in college you and your friends enrolled a fake student, John Smith, and even attended his classes. What prompted that experiment?*

Well, that's not entirely true. John Smith wasn't a fake student, at least not originally. John Smith was a real student who disappeared our freshman year.

*Was he a friend of yours?*

No, none of us were friends with him. He lived in our dorm. Moony, pimply, incredibly hermetic—always in his room, always wearing pajamas. He had taped this note below his doorknob that said, "I'll Be Seeing You." We thought he was sort of creepy. Somehow everyone knew he had a fish tank in his room, even though none of us had ever actually been inside.

But then he disappeared. I don't think he was murdered or kidnapped or anything like that—we would have heard, if that had been the case. A missing person's report or something.

What I do know is that one night—this was on a weekend, everyone was in my room, doing what we always did, which at the time meant a lot of Nintendo and *Strangeways, Here We Come*—anyway these older men came to our dorm and started hauling away his stuff.

By this point we had become sort of obsessed with him. We called him I'll Be Seeing You: that was our codename, in case he ever happened to overhear us talking about him.

*That's a pretty obvious codename, considering he had put that sign on the door himself.*

Well, we thought we were sneaky.

Anyway, someone noticed these people hauling away his stuff—

*Were these uniformed men? A moving company, or something?*

No, no, they were just wearing normal clothes. I'm not sure—is that more suspicious, or less?

But maybe a dozen boxes later, and a few handfuls of hangers, every trace of I'll Be Seeing You was gone. We never actually saw him leave: he must have been gone already, because when the men left, they left the door unlocked, and when we snuck inside, the room was empty.

We'd been obsessed with him for months. We'd been dying to get into his room—we'd even talked about breaking in. But now that we were inside, the room was blank—just carpet, a bare mattress, a desk. It was like traveling to some city you've always wanted to visit, but when you get there, it's been bombed out.

*Did you ever see them carry out the fish tank?*

No, we never did. Maybe it was in one of the boxes, if it actually existed.

Anyway, a few weeks after he disappeared, after we realized he really wasn't coming back, we reenrolled him. Or, we enrolled a new John Smith. The fake one. We were pretty sure he wasn't dead, but just in case he was, we wanted to carry on his existence, in honor of him.

Back then, all you needed was a Social Security number—we made one up—and a few thousand dollars. Everyone in the dorm chipped in. Then we took turns attending his classes, each of us alternatively "becoming" John Smith.

He was a C student.

*The fake John Smith has his own address now—even receives alumni mail. So in some ways he's crossed that boundary between fiction and nonfiction.*

He did fail to attend his commencement ceremony, but that was more of a faux pas than an admission of unreality.

*So it was that incident that got you interested in experimenting with the boundaries between fiction and nonfiction?*

Well, no. There was a similar incident, an earlier incident. Much earlier, before I was even born. I'm not sure how distorted the story's become, having been filtered through a couple generations of Martones. But some of the story is actually documented: birth certificates, newspaper clippings, that sort of thing.

Anyway, my great-grandfather's father wasn't named Martone. He was named Parkhill. He was a cop. This was back when cops carried wood clubs instead of pepper spray, revolvers instead of tasers. And his wife was sleeping with another man, although he didn't know it.

His not knowing was the thing that would have kept us Parkhills, but instead one morning he came home and found them there, his wife and this man, splayed out on his bed. So, he set down his cap, and took out his gun, and then shot himself, right there in front of both of them. My great-grandfather was asleep on a cot down the hall, or at least had been, until he heard it.

And after his father had been buried, his mother married her lover, and my great-grandfather was so ashamed of his father's suicide that he changed his surname—changed it to the stepfather's, the lover's, Martone. So that's who we have been ever since: not the man in the doorway with a gun, but the man in bed, completely naked, afraid of the gun, but only for a second, before he realizes just how the other man's going to use it.

*When did you first hear this story?*

My mother told me when I was about six. My own father had left before I was even one.

But then later I learned that my mother's family had been founded on a fiction of its own. My mother's maiden name was Jeluso, but that great-grandfather had changed his surname too: his father had been involved with the mafia, and had made heaps of money, but my great-grandfather wanted nothing to do with it, with that "blood money." So, to distance himself from all that, he changed his name from Geluso to Jeluso—a minor alteration, but, still, about a change in identity, connected to this shame he felt about things his father had done.

And then in first grade I began to feel that same confusion about identity, but connected to my *own* fathers. My father moved back to town, and I started visiting him on the weekends. But by then my mother had remarried. And for me that was confusing, because now I had two fathers, and they each wore the name "father" at different times. When I was at my father's, I'd call him my "father" and my mother's husband my "stepfather." But when I was home again, I'd call my mother's husband my "father" and him my "biofather."

*"Biofather"?*

"Bio-" as in "biological." That's what we called him around my house, to distinguish between the two. But, it was an odd term: I began to think of myself as some sort of product, as an "offspring" instead of a "child."

Anyway, I was trying to deal with all of these issues. I was a Martone, but really I was a Parkhill, and my mother had been a Jeluso, but really she had been a Geluso, and now she was a Holly, which was my stepfather's surname. And I had this father who was sometimes a father and sometimes a stepfather, and this other father who was sometimes a biofather and sometimes a father. And then later there was that incident with John Smith. So, that's probably what got me interested in pseudonyms, in writing under assumed names: the experiments with Aaron, Hejinian, Bowers, et cetera.

*I've heard about your experiment with Bowers. Neal Bowers had written a memoir called* Words for the Taking, *about his hunt for someone who had plagiarized his poems under the name David Sumner. You then began publishing poems under the name Neal Bowers—donating to his oeuvre, essentially, instead of stealing from it.*

Well, I don't know if I'd call it an oeuvre.

*But what experiments have you done with Hejinian? And Aaron who?*

Shale Aaron. I've published all of Shale Aaron's books, one of Lyn Hejinian's, and three of Thomas Pynchon's.

Aaron is a pseudonym I invented for my speculative fiction. Speculative as in sci-fi: I don't want to tarnish my standing with the "literary" community, so anytime I write something about robots, or cloning, or planets with nine suns, I publish the book under Aaron's name.

Hejinian actually asked me to write a book under her name—she had signed a contract, but then had gone off to Japan for a year, and hadn't written a word. So I published a manuscript I'd been working on under her name. I'd been trying to publish it for almost a year, but no one would touch it. Then suddenly her name was attached to it, and I had eleven different offers.

Later, she contributed a few paragraphs to my story "The English Mercurie, The Historia Augusta."

*Wait, what about Pynchon? You're saying you wrote three of Pynchon's books? Which three?*

Well, yes, only three. But that's because he's a collaboration—I invented Thomas Pynchon along with three other writers, so we have to take turns writing his books. I've written three of his, uh, less-acclaimed novels. I've also written a few of his essays for the *New York Times Book Review*. I don't do any of the blurbs though. Anytime you see a blurb written by Thomas Pynchon, that's not my work—that's one of my collaborators'.

I've also worked as a ghostwriter for Buzz Aldrin under the name Ken Abraham.

*I want to return to what you said about being a Parkhill instead of a Martone. I found that fascinating, partly because I had heard that you were raised in a bilingual home, and I had always assumed the second language was Italian.*

That's actually misleading. I wasn't raised in a bilingual home. What *is* true is that English is my second language.

*But you grew up in Fort Wayne?*

Yes, that rumor's true. But the first few years after I was born I lived at my grandfather's house, which was also in Indiana, but in Delphi, not Fort Wayne. My mother spent those years abroad: apparently the circumstances were such that she felt it would be best to clear out of the country for a while. The details are unclear.

So I was taught the basics of life as a human—how to walk, how to talk, how to flush a toilet—by this eighty-year-old French American with a beard like a lawn gnome's. My grandfather was a retired professor, a scholar of dead languages—he had taught at Purdue. Dalmatian was his obsession. Dalmatian is a Croatian language that's been dead for over a century, but he had spent his whole life studying it, and that was all he spoke at home.

*So your first language was Dalmatian?*

Yes, which really messed me up. Dalmatian is tremendously complicated—it's extinct for a reason. It's an entirely different language system than English, or any of the other Indo-European languages. It has the standard parts of speech: noun, verb, adjective, et cetera. But all the words are gradable. In English, some of our adjectives are gradable. Tall, for example: someone can be tall, or taller, or tallest. Well, in Dalmatian, everything's like that. Like if you were talking about a wolf you saw on television, it'd be either wolf or wolfer or wolfest, depending on how wolf the wolf was. Or if you were talking about how you went running, it'd be something like either you ran or ranner or rannest. In that sense it's actually quite efficient. A tidy language. You only need one run-type verb in Dalmatian: you don't need trot and jog and dash and sprint and a hundred other synonyms that mean the exact same thing but slightly different.

But then try to imagine eating toast or toaster or toastest for breakfast every morning for almost three years, and then your grandfather dies and your mother comes home and when you talk to her, in her language, all you can ask for is toast. What about the days you want toastest? How do you go about trying to explain *that*?

Luckily I was only four—I was able to pick up English fairly quickly. And ultimately the experience was good for me: it forced me to think about the language I was using, to see that there were alternatives to our system, other ways of expressing these different ideas and feelings.

*In an interview with* Granta *you mentioned that for several decades you've been at work on an "interactive" novel, tentatively titled* The Observatory. *How can a novel be "interactive"?*

Did you ever play *Dungeons & Dragons*? When I was a kid I was obsessed with games—my mother taught me mahjong, djambi, shogi, go, and of course we played the newer games like *LIFE* and *Trouble*—but my obsession with *D&D* went beyond any other. And what was so compelling was *D&D* was this narrative game. Other games had this vague sort of narrative attached: in *Clue*, each piece is a named character, and you're trying to solve the murder of Mr. Boddy; in *The Settlers of Catan*, you're building these colonies, warding off pirates. But *D&D* doesn't just have some vague narrative attached—the game is *about* narrative.

*The Observatory* is the opposite. A game-type narrative. Interactive, but chiefly a story.

*As a reader, what's your aesthetic?*

My aesthetic? The aesthetic of the TV dinner, the precooked and flash-frozen, the heat and serve, the shake and bake, the poppin' fresh.

*That's an aesthetic?*

I oppose all forms of irony, sarcasm, apathy, and cynicism. I champion all forms of sincerity, sentimentality, passion, and idealism. I like stories with that same emotional oomph as Hisaishi's "Cave of Mind."

*What have you been reading lately?*

I don't read many books. I spend most of my time reading magazines. *Zoetrope, Subtropics, Transanimation. McSweeney's*, always *McSweeney's*, *McSweeney's* is my obsession.

I did reread *Anna Karenina* earlier this year though.

*Is that a favorite?*

Probably, yes. Partly because my stepfather's parents were farmers.

*Was this also in Indiana?*

No, they lived in Kentucky, near Frankfort. We'd spend holidays there. And my parents would be incredibly bored, just sitting around doing crosswords, trying to bully the television antennas into getting some signal instead of static, but I'd follow my grandfather—my stepgrandfather, but I called him my "grandfather," the same way that I called my stepfather "father"—around everywhere, gathering eggs, feeding the sheep, scrambling around on the haystacks in the barn. He always wore the same camouflage coat, these same rubber boots. I was obsessed with the trivial rituals. With how my grandfather was part of this landscape. He had scars that the farm had left on him: across his knuckles, down a shin. But he'd left his own scars on the farm: scorch marks from bonfires behind the shed, a crater he'd dug to make a pond.

So *Anna Karenina* appeals to that part of me. But what I love is that it's not just about farming. It's this sprawling thing, with all of these ideas stuck in the cracks of it. And what you notice depends on where you're sitting when you're reading it, on which ideas the light catches from your angle.

*What did you see this time?*

Well, I started thinking about how good stories are always about deviants. As soon as someone starts breaking the rules, you've got a good story.

*Kiss of the Spider Woman* has this potential to be incredibly boring—just these two guys sitting around talking, for two hundred pages, that's all it is. But a few pages in, you realize they're sitting in a prison cell, and you're hooked. They've done something wrong. You want to know what. You're wondering if they're going to do other things, break other rules.

But what's deviant is defined by culture, by our laws, our social norms. So our best stories wouldn't translate for a culture where, say, adultery was the norm. *Anna Karenina*'s appeal is that Anna is doing something we consider taboo. For a polyamorous society, you could translate the words, but the story itself would get lost along the way.

But that's the allure of a story—it allows you to live out a fantasy, something you want to do that you can't or wouldn't do in your own life. You can't write a story where everyone is just doing laundry, sending greeting cards to each other. Someone has to steal the laundry from the laundromat; someone has to refuse to sign the greeting card.

*But we're* Kiss of the Spider Woman: *"Just these two guys sitting around talking." Who's going to want to read this? What's the allure of the author interview?*

Well, writers are deviants. Readers know this. The allure of the author interview is that readers are hoping I'll admit to having done some bizarre or shocking thing. And, for the sake of the interview, I will.

But not yet. I want to talk about more books. Then I'll tell you which rules I've broken.

*I'm curious which writers you feel have influenced your own writing.*

Borges, whom I've written a lot about. Holst's *The Planets*, Biber's *Sonata representativa*. Makoto Shinkai, Katsuhiro Otomo, Masashi Kishimoto. I've also been—well, this isn't going to make any sense. I'm not sure how to explain this theory. I would name Jesse Ball as an influence, but you'd say, that doesn't make any sense, he's only just started publishing books, he's like thirty years old. But it's a mistake to think that we can only be influenced by existent texts. I have a theory that my *Pensées* was hugely influenced by Ball's *The Way Through Doors*, and that *Pensées* in turn was hugely influential on Barthelme's *The Dead Father*.

*How does that work?*

I also really admire David Foster Wallace. Writing an experimental story, that's one thing: anyone can think of a clever gimmick. But in Wallace's stories, the gimmick *was never just a gimmick*. The gimmick was always tied to the content of the story—was necessary, somehow crucial to the telling of the story itself. And that's something very difficult to do.

Another writer who's done that is Damon Galgut. Have you read his story "The Lover"? It's narrated by this man who traveled through Africa a number of years ago and then joined up with these Europeans and fell in love with this other man. But throughout the story, the narrator alternates between referring to himself in the first person, as a "me," and third person, as a "he." Which on its own is just a gimmick—sure, it's clever, it's an experiment with these different narrative modes. But "The Lover" is all about this distance the narrator feels with who he was when he made this trip: it feels like a separate self from the self he is now. And that's what the gimmick does—the gimmick makes you *feel* that. You're going back and forth between these "me" and "he" moments, and that makes you really feel the distance, this sense that, when he did certain things he did, he was a stranger to the self he is now.

*I've heard you also read a lot of graphic novels.*

I'm obsessed with all forms of storytelling: comics, film, opera, sculpture, puppetry, video games. Every form has certain capabilities unique to that form alone. And, at the same time, certain incapabilities. That's what interests me: learning to exploit whatever medium I'm working in. Film, for example, has a number of capabilities the stage doesn't have, although early filmmakers didn't exploit this: it wasn't until later films like *Battleship Potemkin* and *Citizen Kane* that filmmakers began manipulating the audience's perspective in ways that would have been impossible on the stage. *Memento* is another film that exploits its medium—achieves certain things, visually, that would be impossible to do in a novel. And, again, it's more than a gimmick: *Memento* exploits its medium to produce a certain effect, an effect crucial to its telling.

But you asked about graphic novels. Well, Chris Ware has made the same breakthroughs with comics that Eisenstein and Welles once made with film. Have you read *Jimmy Corrigan*? *Jimmy Corrigan* contains one two-page spread that would be entirely irreproducible in any other medium. It doesn't matter how talented a writer or filmmaker or choreographer you are: those two pages of *Jimmy Corrigan* make narrative leaps that are only possible in comics. In them Ware explores the form of the diagram—the same sort of diagram you might use to put together a cabinet, or repair the engine of a truck—and uses it to reveal about two hundred years' worth of story. It couldn't be done with words: it would take at least a chapter, if not a novel, to cover the territory Ware does in those two pages. Film is probably the closest medium to comics, in that film combines images and words—through sound instead of print—but even with film you couldn't do it. In Ware's spread, the story is in how the separate images are arranged on the page, and the ways that Ware connects them.

Michael Martone *is a collection of fictional contributor's notes;* The Blue Guide to Indiana *is a fictional travel guide, parts of which were published as nonfiction in newspapers and magazines; and some of your essays, such as "I, Libertine" and "Naked Came the Stranger," are composed almost entirely of excerpts lifted from other texts. What's the reader meant to take away from projects like these?*

A few years ago there was this controversy: a high school science teacher decided to devote a whole month to teaching his students about a made-up dinosaur. And then he held an exam. The students had spent a whole month memorizing details about this dinosaur: its bone structure, its nesting habits, the fact that it had evolved during the Triassic Period of the Mesozoic Era. For weeks these students crammed—studied flash cards, invented mnemonic devices, fell asleep repeating information about the dinosaur. And then they took the test. And the students who got 5/10, he failed them. The students who got 6/10, or 7/10, or 8/10, or 9/10, he failed them. The students who got 10/10—the students who got *every question right*—he failed them. The whole class failed the test.

The only correct answer, he said, was, "This dinosaur never existed." But none of them had written that. Because none of them had bothered to look up the dinosaur on their own.

The point was that his students should question what he's saying, not just memorize everything they're told without thinking. And of course his students fought it, because they didn't think they should be failed for passing a test, and their parents fought it, because they didn't think he should have wasted a whole month of the school year on an imaginary dinosaur.

But that was the spirit of *The Blue Guide to Indiana*. We treat our media like ninth-grade science teachers: we swallow everything without questioning a word. And of course there were complaints: I got calls from people who were confused, because they had driven fifteen hours to see the Field of Lightbulbs, and it wasn't there. But that's what the book was about—teaching people to read journalism discerningly, even travel articles. "If you see a 'buffalo' sign on an elephant's cage, do not trust your eyes."

Even you, right now. You shouldn't just be sitting there with your phone in your hands, recording me. You should be asking yourself: Can I believe him? Is that true? And I should be doing the same thing. I should be asking: Can I believe you? Can I believe what you're saying?

*I'm only asking questions. They're interrogative, not declarative. Can a question be a lie?*

Was that high school production of *Twelfth Night* your first time playing Shakespeare? Which role did you play?

*...?*

Did you ever actually act in a production of *Twelfth Night*?

*No, I don't do well on stage.*

But my questions implied that you had—assumed certain things about you, in a "declarative" way, while doing their "interrogative" work. Anyone eavesdropping would have assumed that you *had* acted in a high school production of *Twelfth Night*, at least until you responded to the questions. But that's also possible with declarative statements: I could say, "I've heard you played Cesario," but you could still say, "No, I was Viola," or, "No, I was never in that play."

It's up to you, and anyone eavesdropping, to determine whether anything I say—whether it be interrogative, declarative, imperative, or exclamatory—is factual or misleading. And then—is it intentionally misleading, or unintentionally? Am I dishonest, or simply misinformed?

These are the same questions we're supposed to ask when we're reading fiction: our job is to determine whether the narrator is reliable or unreliable. But we forget how much of life beyond novels is also fictional.

*Borges wrote about that sort of thing: I'm thinking of "The Theme of the Traitor and the Hero."*

Well, that's even trickier. What Borges argues in that story is that even things that *actually happen* can be a fiction. In the story, this band of revolutionaries in Poland discovers that their leader is a traitor: he's been collaborating with the government. But the people of Poland idolize him, and the revolutionaries are terrified of what will happen if he's exposed as a traitor—the people will lose faith in the revolution, the revolution will collapse.

So, during the months leading up to the revolution, the revolutionaries use Warsaw as a theater. By now the traitor has agreed to cooperate. They speak certain lines to him at certain times; he's given certain items, including a sealed letter; he's paraded around Warsaw, creating memories still treasured by the people of Poland. Then, on the eve of the revolution, they kill him—as with the other scenes in their drama, they perform the murder in a public setting. And the people of Poland assume he was assassinated, by the government. So, the traitor becomes a hero, this rallying point for the people, instead of a point of shame. The narrator of the story uncovers all of this: he's been researching the story of the traitor, who happens to be his great-grandfather. But when he learns the truth, he decides to perpetuate the fiction: he writes a book glorifying the traitor, becoming, himself, part of the fiction, just playing another role in the play.

*What projects are you working on now?*

I'm learning to exploit my own medium—the written story—in the same way Ware learned to exploit his. The written story evolved from the oral tradition, and like that early relationship between film and the stage, we often write our stories like we're just telling them out loud. Which is fine, to a certain extent. But I'm interested in writing stories that couldn't possibly be told in any other medium: written stories, in other words, that couldn't be translated into film, or comics, or even spoken out loud, without losing some fundamental part of themselves.

Like footnotes, for example. But I don't want to use footnotes just because footnotes happen to be this thing you can only use on the page. I want to use footnotes in some way that's crucial to my story. I want my story to be *realized* by its footnotes—not just a mannequin for putting the footnotes on display.

I've also been writing articles for Wikipedia.

*Fictional? Or nonfictional?*

Well, fictional. But it's not mean spirited. I don't vandalize the articles. I fictionalize the articles to match their content with fictions that I've created in reality. Similar to the narrator in that story by Borges. For example, I've contributed to Thomas Pynchon's article. If I were to write a nonfictional article—that Pynchon is a pseudonym shared by four different writers—someone else would just come along and change it anyway. So instead I supply the details that the fiction requires, now that it has become, to a certain extent, nonfictional: that he studied at Cornell, was in the Navy, et cetera.

*But, again, an interactive narrative, which other editors now help to shape. What attracts you to those sorts of fictions?*

I've always admired the video game as a medium for storytelling, that interactive quality especially. Video game designers have to do a certain amount of storytelling: create the world, write a plot. But a lot of the storytelling is left up to the person playing the game. Take *Final Fantasy VII*. I didn't mention this earlier, for similar reasons why I use Shale Aaron as a pseudonym when I'm writing about robots, but to a certain extent there isn't any story that's influenced my life as much as *Final Fantasy VII*. Anyway, in *Final Fantasy VII* the game will say something like: next you have to go to the town of Nibelheim to inspect an abandoned reactor. But you don't actually have to do that. You can go to Fort Condor looking for someone to trade some item, or go to the Gold Saucer and race chocobos for a few hours, or go to Bugenhagen's observatory and just stand there a while in the holographic planets. The storytelling is interactive: the creators give you the pieces, but you can assemble the story however you see fit. The only time I've ever seen this done with printed stories is the *Choose Your Own Adventure* series. But I'm interested in finding other ways to write interactive stories, to create that on the page: stories more like a menu, or a puzzle, than a traditional narrative. Stories that act like a Rubik's cube—where there is a correct way to read it, but where it's up to the reader to twist the shape of it, to rearrange its pieces until everything lines up. And where, even if you can't figure it out, and just leave it all jumbled, there are still all of these bright colors on the surface.

# AN INTERVIEW WITH MICHAEL MARTONE

Depending on whom you ask, Michael Martone is either contemporary literature's most notorious prankster, innovator, or mutineer. In 1985 his AAP membership was briefly revoked after Martone published his first two books—a "prose" collection titled *Alive and Dead in Indiana* and a "poetry" collection titled *Safety Patrol*—which, aside from *Safety Patrol*'s line breaks, were word-for-word identical. His membership to the Irish Writers Union was revoked in 1999 after IWU discovered that, while Martone's registered nom de plume had been "born" in the village of Castlebridge, Martone himself never even had been to Ireland. His AWP membership was revoked in 2007, reinstated in 2008, and revoked again in 2010.

After his first two books, Martone went on to write *Michael Martone*, a collection of fictional contributor's notes originally published among nonfictional contributor's notes in cooperative journals; *The Blue Guide to Indiana*, a collection of travel articles reviewing fictional attractions such as the Musee de Axl Rose and the memorial to the Indianapolis Dairy Prohibition of 1971 (most of which were, again, originally published as nonfiction); fictional interviews with his mentor Philip Roth; fictional advertisements in the margins of magazines such as *The Atlantic* and *Ploughshares*; poems under the names of nonfictional colleagues; and blurbs for nonexistent books.

But his latest book is perhaps the most revealing: *Racing in Place* is a collection of essays exploring his obsession with gas masks, welding helmets, flash gear, and face shields, symbols of "these kinds of workplace anonymity." Born in Fort Wayne, Indiana, Martone is often described as an anthropologist, and his cultural concerns mirror his literary: he has argued humankind historically "[keeps] the same systems, but [gives] them new disguises."

Martone now lives in Tuscaloosa, where he teaches in the MFA program at the University of Alabama. For our interview, Martone booked us tickets for a performance of *Vortigern and Rowena* at the historic Bama Theater. However, when I arrived I discovered that Martone had booked us in separate, albeit neighboring, boxes.

During each act of the play Martone curtained his box so as to screen it from my own. Thus, this interview was conducted during the play's two intermissions, when his box was uncurtained. It's also worth noting that I had never met Martone before our interview, but had written to him that I would be "the one wearing white suspenders and a purple bow tie." When I arrived, Martone also was wearing white suspenders and a purple bow tie. When I commented on this, Martone said only that he had thought it would be "cute to match."

*You've published fictional "nonfiction" in a variety of media: "Document 12-571-3570," "The Voice of Vrillon." What first got you interested in experimenting with those boundaries between fiction and nonfiction?*

When I was a kid, I lived for a while with my uncle and my cousin Maddie. My uncle was an alcoholic. He was a very kind and happy drunk, but still he was drunk just about every night. At breakfast he'd drink a pot of coffee, four or five mugfuls before leaving for work, and when he got home again he'd rinse the dried coffee grounds out of his mug, uncork a bottle of wine, and then drink four or five mugfuls of that.

Living with an alcoholic, I became obsessed with this binary opposition of "sober" and "drunk." I thought about it all of the time. When did my sober uncle become my drunk uncle? When was that *exact moment?*

My obsession with that binary opposition of "fiction" and "nonfiction" developed in a similar way. As an undergraduate student I lived in the dorms every year, and every year I roomed with a different pathological liar.

*Intentionally?*

No, it wasn't intentional. With each roommate, I never realized he was a pathological liar until we were already living together.

*That can't have been entirely coincidental: four in a row, all with the same compulsion?*

Actually, it was five. And I'm sure it wasn't a coincidence. My freshman year I went in blind, so my rooming with a liar that year could have been a coincidence. But my befriending a pathological liar from Connecticut and living with him my sophomore year? Then befriending a pathological liar from Queens and living with him my junior year? Then befriending pathological liars from Georgia and Wyoming and living with them my senior year? It *was* unintentional, but it wasn't coincidental. Something obviously attracted me to pathological liars.

I suspect it was their stories: they could tell a story better than anyone else on campus. And they could do that because they weren't limited to nonfiction—or even creative nonfiction. When other kids talked about their weekends, you got journalism, you got the news. But when my friends talked about their weekends, you got fiction—or at least autobiographical fiction.

And I guess I preferred the fiction. Jane Yolen has this essay where she says, "Story is the best kind of lie-telling. It exaggerates the real, replaces it with something larger and more imaginative in order to illuminate our somewhat smaller lives." But maybe the opposite is also true: maybe lie-telling is the best kind of story.

*And you knew your sophomore, junior, and senior roommates before living with them?*

Yes, to different degrees.

*How could you have failed to notice, again and again, your friends' compulsions?*

You don't understand. For them, lying wasn't some sort of hobby. It was how they lived—in their fictions, *every second of every minute of every hour of every day.* Their survival, socially, depended on their ability to deceive those closest to them: their families, their friends, their classmates and professors.

With someone that devoted to their fictions, you won't notice the lies they're telling unless you're spending five, seven, eleven hours of the day with them—in other words, unless you're living together. Even the most experienced liars will slip up when their guard is down, but that's only maybe a few times a day:

when they're pouring their cereal, or digging for socks in their hamper, or still groggy from a nap.

With my freshman roommate, Bowers, it was this story he liked to tell about a fight he had gotten into at a frat party—that was how he slipped up.

*What gave him away?*

Bowers was this very hip bearded fellow who shopped exclusively at thrift stores and smoked clove cigarettes. Or maybe it would be more accurate to say that he *thought* he was very hip. What's indisputable is he was bearded.

On weekends Bowers and his friends liked to go to frat parties and steal beer from the frats' refrigerators and dance around the frats' basements as weirdly as possible. It was about disturbing the sorority girls and irritating the fraternity boys. Bowers and his friends thought this was really funny. They did this every weekend for months, and months, and months.

Anyway, one Sunday at the cafeteria Bowers had this story about how he and his friends—they were all older, so they ate off campus, never with us—about how he and his friends had almost gotten into a fight at this party. Bowers said he'd been doing his usual half-squirming half-convulsing dance when this senior lounging against the boiler—this senior's name was Charles Dodgson, about whom I knew nothing except that supposedly his friends hated him even more than the rest of the campus, which was a lot, but still had to spend just about every waking second of their lives with him because he'd gotten hazed into the same frat—Dodgson grabbed Bowers by the collar of his sweater and started yelling at him. "Get the fuck out of here, you fucking faggot"—your standard frat-house parlance. But some other kids in the fraternity got between them and broke up the fight before he could take a swing at Bowers. Basically, there was a lot of yelling, and then Bowers and his friends got kicked out.

*And you knew the story was a lie?*

No, the story wasn't a lie—all of that had actually happened. "Even an oyster has enemies."

But Bowers loved telling stories. It was how he made so many friends: he was always telling stories about himself. Not stories that necessarily made him out to be heroic, or clever, or anything—he had one story he'd tell about pissing himself in front of his entire second grade class—but *good stories*.

And here's why they were so good. Being his roommate, I had to hear that story about the party over and over and over—whenever we ran into someone Bowers hadn't told it to yet. And on Monday he was telling it to some people, and an interesting thing happened. In the story, when Dodgson grabbed Bowers and started shouting, a minor character appeared in the background: a man with an empty bottle. Now sure, you could say, maybe Bowers just hadn't bothered to mention the man with the bottle before—that doesn't mean the man was a fiction.

But people liked the man with the bottle: they leaned in when he appeared, were asking questions about him, were laughing. So in Tuesday's tellings, the man with the bottle became a major character. The man was sort of menacing Bowers—the Bowers in the story—with the bottle, as if he were going to hurt him with it. In Wednesday's tellings the man with the bottle was still there, and in one of Thursday's tellings the man with bottle *broke the bottle against the wall and held it at his throat.*

The story always ended the same way: the fight got broken up, Bowers and his friends got kicked out. But the story's plot had changed.

Of course, this revision happened over the course of a dozen, a few dozen tellings. Even listening to every telling, the changes were so subtle, it was almost impossible to tell anything was changing. But if you had listened to his first version of the story, and if you had listened to the version he was telling by Thursday, you'd say, wait—where'd the broken bottle come from?

I felt sorry for Bowers, because I honestly think he wasn't even aware of his lie-telling. I think his revision process was so careful and so patient, not just to safeguard against getting caught, but as a way of revising *the memory itself.* When Bowers told people about the broken bottle, he thought that bottle *really had been there.* He *believed* he had experienced that glass against his throat. A man like that, he corrupts all of his memories: everything he remembers having happened to him simply didn't. He thinks he's lived a certain kind of life, when he's actually lived a duller one, a lonelier one, a life where the bottles are never broken.

*So then you signed up to live with someone else your sophomore year. And even after living with Bowers, you didn't realize this other kid was also a liar?*

They were different genres of liars. Did you know there are different genres? Maybe you didn't.

Bowers was a realist: he only lied about things that had actually happened. Realists are the most devious liars. They're almost impossible to unmask. They don't just lie: they exaggerate the truth, and then exaggerate the exaggeration, and then exaggerate that, and *that's* the lie.

My sophomore roommate, Neal, was an absurdist—told lies that weren't based on any reality whatsoever. Neal had performed as a backup dancer in famous hip-hop videos. In order to join us at Indiana University he'd had to decline offers both to golf professionally and to play in the NHL. He'd vacationed with Updike. His parents had bought him a penguin for Christmas. Et cetera. He'd died once, he told us.

Neal knew he was lying. I felt sorry for him not because he didn't realize he was lying, but because he didn't realize that *we* knew he was lying. He actually thought we believed him, believed everything. After a while, we didn't believe *anything* he said, anything at all.

My junior-year roommate was a realist again, and my senior-year roommates were humorists: they'd tell lies that they meant to be found out. They thought tricking you was funny, but if you didn't catch on, they'd come out and tell you. They wanted to trick you, but the routine wasn't fun for them if the lies weren't ever exposed, if you didn't end up laughing too.

Their genre was harmless. I loved living with humorists. But the others I came to hate.

*In an interview with* Granta *you revealed that lately you've been at work on "fictions even shorter than flash fiction: fictions as quick as a phrase, or even a word." What did you mean, exactly, "or even a word"?*

Fictional fortunes, for example. About the size of fortune-cookie fortunes, but handwritten.

*You publish these?*

No. I just hide them, somewhere, for strangers to find—tucked under a pepper shaker, into the pocket of an unsold jacket, et cetera. I don't keep copies. I'll write one, "publish" it between the slats of a bench, then write another. *He's only stalking you because he loves you.* I published that walking here, in the basket of a bicycle chained to a porch. *Expect to suffer a nonlethal infection later this month.* That was in a window box, in among the tulips. *A family heirloom is at risk of theft. Rewire your lamps or risk a housefire. You would be happier in Arkansas.* Into random programs in the lobby.

*Grim fortunes.*

"I try to make everyone's day a little more surreal."

After my uncle died, I inherited an airplane, a 1977 Titan II model. Ever since then, I've been experimenting with the sky as a medium, too, self-publishing different phrases.

*Skywriting? Like "EAT AT MICHAEL'S"? That kind of thing?*

Skywriting was actually invented in Fort Wayne, by a stunt pilot named Art Smith. Smith Field, in Fort Wayne, is named for him. He also inspired the founding of Honda, the motor company, totally accidentally. At the age of twelve, Soichiro Honda stole a bicycle and pedaled two hours to see this stunt show. He couldn't afford the admission fee, though, was turned out. But he had never seen an airplane before. He was determined. So he snuck into a tree. There, from those branches, Honda saw Smith looping through the clouds—two tons of metal, somehow *suspended in the sky*—and fell in love with machines.

Anyway, for a skywriter, "EAT AT MICHAEL'S" would be cliché, of course. Instead, I'm writing serial fiction: I publish messages between fictional characters, which together build a traditional narrative. A romance, of sorts, for my audience on the ground.

*The fortune-telling, the skywriting, those aren't as short as "even a word," though.*

Well, the past few years, I've also been working as a lexicographer, writing ghost words for dictionaries. "Even a word," that's what that meant.

*"Ghost words"?*

Concerning plagiarism, publishing companies are basically militant, consider anybody with a printing machine "a potential plagiarist." Dictionary publishers especially: they have these nightmares about people flipping through their dictionaries, copying the definitions, and then cranking out their own. And they have those nightmares because, with dictionaries, tracking that sort of thing can be difficult. When lexicographers write a definition for a word, they're not creating: they're describing some abstract idea that already exists in the collective consciousness of English speakers. When lexicographers write a definition for the word *medium*, they're all defining the same *medium*. Like a bunch of painters doing portraits of the same face—painters who, by the nature of their project, have to paint that face as realistically as possible. Overlap is inevitable, theft difficult to prove.

So, the lexicographers write ghost words: fictional words with fictional definitions. *Heenless*, for example, an adjective I defined as "lacking the ability to recognize truths revealed by a fiction." Including ghost words in a dictionary doesn't undermine its credibility, obviously. People only use a dictionary to look up a certain word. They look their word up, and that's that. Nobody's going to look up *heenless*, because *heenless* doesn't exist. But if *heenless* shows up in another dictionary, then my publisher will know that we've been ripped off: *heenless* could have come only from our dictionary.

I couldn't have written *heenless* if I had never met my roommates. Before living with them, I *was* heenless. Living with them, though, I realized their lies did reveal certain truths: when they lied, the lie would teach me something about their childhoods, or about the Midwest, or about capitalism, or whatever. Sometimes the lie would teach me something about myself.

*Who publishes these "ghost words"?*

I've been writing for *Merriam-Webster, OED, OAD, American Heritage,* et cetera. Eventually I'll publish a collection, but so far, as a logodaedalus, I've only written about a hundred words.

But I consider ghost words a form of storytelling. I try to write words that have some narrative quality—either in the word itself, or in the definition. Ghost words are to flash fiction what flash fiction is to the short story and what the short story is to the novel. The shorter the fiction, the more difficult it becomes to tell a compelling story. But occasionally I succeed.

*Have you been experimenting with any other new forms?*

I've also been using the dream as a medium for storytelling. To do that, though, I had to develop the ability to lucid dream, which for me was an enormous struggle.

*By "lucid dream," do you mean an especially vivid dream, or something?*

No, a lucid dream is when, while dreaming, you become *aware* that you're dreaming. Typically becoming aware would eject you from the dream—would wake you up—but if you can manage to stay in it, you can actually control it. You can *write the dream*: alter the plot, change the scene, introduce new characters, write your dialogue, write *everyone's* dialogue.

It's unpublishable, obviously: I can't share the dreams I write with anyone. But that doesn't, to me, mean they're not worthwhile.

*How did you develop the ability to lucid dream?*

To lucid dream, your dream recall has to average between five to seven nights a week—

*"Dream recall"?*

Your ability to remember your dreams upon waking. My dream recall used to average about once a month. In other words, was just abysmal.

To improve your average, the dream scholar Hervey de Saint-Denys suggests recording your dreams every morning. Making notes every morning forms a habit: Saint-Denys believed if you went into your dreams with the intent to remember, you were much more likely to do so.

*Did that work for you?*

Within weeks my dream recall had improved, and after a few months I was remembering my dreams almost nightly.

*But how did you induce the lucid dreams, then?*

Again, my method was stolen from Saint-Denys. His method was to carry a thumb piano everywhere. The habit of carrying it led to it appearing in his dreams—but in his dreams, when he played it, the sound was "a music that was not music." This nightmarish, otherworldly sound that he knew couldn't come out of a thumb piano. Which is how he knew that he was dreaming.

The only thumb pianos I could find in Tuscaloosa were unwieldy and overpriced, so I opted to carry around a harmonica instead—that's what I use to write my dreams.

*Has your "storytelling" while dreaming had any impact on your writing?*

Sometimes my writing process will require a lucid dream. My story "Metempsychosis," for example: I got stuck, while writing that, at this certain scene. I was halfway through the story and knew where it would end but didn't know how to get it there.

So I took the scene into my dreams. I was dreaming that my cousin Maddie and I were in some factory, on a conveyer belt, with a bunch of other people, getting carried toward a pit. When I became aware that I was dreaming, however, I assumed control. I emptied the dream of its characters, instead brought in the characters from my story—Joaquin, Rafael, Leaf, the gloomy moonshiners, the mangy dog. I moved everyone from the factory to the setting of my story—suddenly we were standing there in the alley of that fishing village along the shore of Lake Erie, with the "pale starlight" I had written into the scene, the "square windows with diamond panes," the "wisps of snow returning to the earth like bright scraps of joy."

And then I made Joaquin say what he was supposed to say, and then I made the dog bark how he was supposed to bark, and then I did nothing. I watched, waiting. Even when you're lucid dreaming, your subconscious can still affect what's happening. And, as I watched, my subconscious assumed control and wrote the rest of the dream for me.

When I woke up I wrote down the gist of what had happened, and then ate some oatmeal, and then spent the rest of the day in my sunroom, writing that scene from my dream into "Metempsychosis." I don't know if it was the perfect story, with that scene my subconscious had given me, but it was a story, and before my dream I'd had only half of that.

*What stories have influenced your fiction?*

Conceptually? The video game *Chain World*. Formally? The video games *Journey, Braid, Fez.*

*In "Pediophobia" you said you rank fiction by your degree of jealousy: the "best" fiction being the fiction that produces, in you, the greatest feelings of jealousy, of wishing you had made it.*

I recently visited Rome, in Italy, to bail my sons from a local prison. While there, I visited the Mouth of Truth. Have you seen the Mouth of Truth? It's this giant marble sculpture, cracking apart, with the image of a man's face. Round, like the Man in the Moon. Holes for eyes, holes for nostrils, a gaping mouth. You can stick your hands in the mouth: it's that large. And there's a rumor that, if you tell a lie while your hands are in the mouth, the mouth will bite off your hands.

There are books I'm jealous of: *Middlesex, Anthem, Dune, Cloud Atlas*. I'm jealous of the films *Haeven, Biutiful*. I'm jealous of the manga *Fullmetal Alchemist*, the anime *Cowboy Bebop*. I'm jealous of the video game *Myst*. But my jealousy for the Mouth of Truth, for that rumor, outweighs my jealousy for any published fiction. What a powerful, addicting story! *If you lie, this mouth will eat your hands.*

I didn't visit the sculpture alone. After bailing my sons from prison, I took my sons. I made them put their hands into the mouth, I told them the legend, and then I asked them a question. "Did you steal what they said you did?" My sons stared at their arms, up to their wrists in the mouth. The story had frightened them. They couldn't lie to me. They wanted to keep their hands. "Sorry, but, yes," they said.

Those are the stories that captivate people, that truly change people, that shake people to the core. Myths, rumors, legends. Those are the fictions that produce, in me, "the greatest feelings of jealousy." Each year, hundreds of thousands visit the Mouth of Truth. People enchanted, somehow touched, by an anonymous rumor.

Likewise, of my own fictions, I'm proudest of my rumors.

*Rumors?*

Each year, I travel all over the country: attending conferences, visiting relatives, sightseeing. This year, I visited Eugene, Oregon; Franklin, Louisiana; Kent, Washington; Warren, Arizona; and five Madisons—Maine's, Tennessee's, Mississippi's, New Jersey's, and New Hampshire's—all in the span of a month. And, whenever I'm walking through a city with somebody, I'll always stop to make up a story. "I've heard…" I'll say, pointing at an abandoned bridge over some river, "that's that bridge where, if you kiss the railing on a certain night, you'll remember something you've forgotten." Or, "Isn't that..." I'll say, pointing at a lighthouse on some pier, "the spot where, if you whisper the worst thing you've ever done, the ghosts of all of the children who've drowned there will appear?"

*...And that works?*

That's where myths come from. An actual person at an actual moment *inventing a story*. The rumor doesn't always catch, but if the story's compelling enough, the rumor will spread.

Those are the works I'm proudest of. My masterpieces. Lost roads, cursed warehouses, vanishing hitchhikers, ghost roller coasters. Maybe half the haunted mansions in this country are my own inventions. The last time I crossed that bridge in Austin, I counted eleven different smears of lipstick on the railing.

*What genre of liar does that make you?*

Rumorer? Fabulist? Mythmaker?

*Some reviewers have described you as "exoliterary."*

I don't like labels like those. I don't like labels period. "Prose," "poetry." "Fiction," "nonfiction." They don't seem useful to me—they seem restricting. I'm hesitant even to identify myself as "Michael Martone," let alone start classifying what species of writer "Michael Martone" is.

*You've said you don't think of yourself as a "self," but as a "democracy of cells."*

Honestly, sometimes it's an anarchy.

*A literary taxonomy is useful to booksellers, at least, in marketing their books to readers.*

Sure, the labels are useful to Amazon. But for writers they're just a means of telling us what we can and can't do. We have these categories: "fiction" and "nonfiction." Now that those have been established, those are your two options. You can write a fictional book or you can write a nonfictional book. Even if your fictional book contains some nonfiction—and it has to, it can't not—you're still required to pretend, "This is a work of fiction. Names, characters, places, and incidents are a product of the author's imagination. Any resemblance to actual persons, living or dead, events, or locales is entirely coincidental." And if your nonfictional book contains some fiction—and, again, it can't not—you'll get flayed alive if anyone bothers to notice. See: the media-held execution of James Frey.

"Fiction," "nonfiction," are just the opposite sides of a Möbius strip. Have you seen a Möbius strip? A Möbius strip appears to have two sides, *but both sides are the same side.* Science textbooks from the 1950s contain information now considered totally fictional, while sci-fi books from the same decade contain fictional inventions no longer fictional but real.

*I'd argue that books can be wholly fictional, or wholly nonfictional.*

Here's the calculus. The function for this is f(x) = 1/x. Do you know that function? Here, give me your program, and I'll draw you the graph. Positive values only. Okay. See? These lines, this crossbeam here, are your x axis and your y axis. And f(x), that line here, curves between the axes. My graph is sloppy, so just google "f(x) = 1/x" when you get home. Anyway, in this direction the function seems to end up overlapping the x axis, and in that direction the function seems to end up overlapping the y axis, right? But here's the thing. No matter how small or how large a value you plug in for x, the line *never actually touches either axis.* It just comes so close that, to the human eye, it's impossible to tell that it's not touching.

*So the line swings from the x axis to the y axis, but will never actually touch either.*

Right. So for this analogy, the x axis is our abstract concept of "fiction" and the y axis is our abstract concept of "nonfiction." And this line here, f(x), is literature. Any story ever written, you can plot as a point somewhere along the line. Most are in that dip around x = 1: *The Sun Also Rises,* which is about equal parts fiction and nonfiction; *A Heartbreaking Work of Staggering Genius,* which is about equal parts nonfiction and fiction; Yoknapatawpha County, from the fictional novels by William Faulkner, which was populated by people taken from a nonfictional diary by Francis Leak. Others, though, are so close to that x axis or that y axis, to being totally fiction or totally nonfiction, that to the human eye there is no discernible difference.

But every fiction makes use of at least some truths: gravity, for example, which is nonfictional, and which has been used in every novel I've ever read. For a story to be totally fictional and actually *touch* that x axis, the story would need to, A) be written in an entirely fictional language, B) be set in an entirely fictional universe—not some version of our universe, like *Star Wars*, but an entirely fictional universe, with its own systems of mathematics, its own laws of physics, its own units of matter, all distinct from ours, and beings that experience that universe through imaginary senses instead of actual senses like sight—and C) as usual, be about entirely fictional characters. In other words, a true work of fiction would be incomprehensible. Paul French's *Untitled* comes closest, probably, but still never touches that axis.

Or take the other end of the spectrum: nonfiction. Take, for example, second-grader Michael Martone describing an incident at a bus stop, which I once had to do. Michael may be under the impression that he's telling nonfiction, telling "the truth." But because he wasn't in a position to hear what the bus driver was saying inside the bus while the incident was happening, or to have seen what was happening on the other side of the school bus at the moment of the incident, or to have seen the snowman that some of the other children built that morning, Michael's interpretation of the events will always be at least somewhat flawed—if not totally off-base—and therefore partly a fiction. Hejinian writes about this in *My Life*: "There were more storytellers than there were stories, so that everyone in the family had a version of history and it was impossible to get close to the original, or to know 'what really happened.'" As the sensory experiences of any single person are limited by the perspective of that person, for a story to be totally nonfictional and actually *touch* that y axis, the story would need to be written by everyone who ever existed and exists and will exist. A recording of the collective human experience. But, then again, that would be limited to a human perspective, so might still be considered a fiction, in that we as a species are also probably operating under certain misconceptions.

*Those seem like excessively rigorous standards for "fiction" and "nonfiction."*

In *Dreams and How to Guide Them*, Saint-Denys says, "We see nothing in dreams that we have not seen before." Saint-Denys had been studying his dreams since he was thirteen, and in his studies he had observed that nothing appeared in his dreams that he had not seen while awake, that he *could not dream* of something that wasn't taken from a memory.

That's not to say Saint-Denys never dreamed about anything unusual or fantastic or bizarre—black flowers blooming on white trees, fire-breathing schoolchildren, the dead digging graves for the living into the undersides of clouds—but he recognized that images like these were simply his memories dismantled, rearranged, and recombined. He had never seen white trees with black flowers, for example, but he had seen trees with flowers and the color white and the color black and his imagination had fused all of that into this image that appeared to be something new. His imagination could only form images from memories: it couldn't invent its own images. What he could not dream was trees of a new color—of a color he had never seen.

Which is why labels like "fiction" and "nonfiction" seem problematic. You can't write a "fictional" character—Hemingway can't write Robert Jordan—unless you're using memories of nonfictional people to create that character. And when you write about "nonfictional" events, you're using a limited vocabulary to describe perished memories, memories that were flawed even when they were fresh, memories that were limited by your own perspective.

But if we are going to keep using labels like "fiction" and "nonfiction," I think we should have a third label, which is why I wrote *diffiction*.

*Is that a new story?*

No, *diffiction* is from my series of ghost words. I defined *diffiction* as "a memory inconsistent with the shared reality of others' memories; something nonfictional to an individual but fictional to that individual's society."

*So an instance of diffiction might be, for example, a schizophrenic's memory of being pursued by government agents in unmarked vans?*

That's an extreme example. We're subjected to commonplace *diffictions* every day. Hejinian writes about this, too, in *My Life*: "My old uncle entertained us with his lie, a story about an event in his childhood, a catastrophe in a sailboat that never occurred, but he was blameless, unaccountable, since, in the course of the telling he had come to believe the lie himself." Or like that story "The Other Death." I love Borges's stories, memorize lines from them as if they were poems. The narrator in that story says, "He talked about Capgras, Fortsas, Bilitis, and did so with such perfectly formed periods, and so vividly, that I realized that he'd told these same stories many times before—indeed, it all made me fear that behind his words hardly any memories remained." Our memories spoil easily, go rotten with time.

*Diffiction* is my most successful work, of the neologisms, in that since its publication it's appeared in new dictionaries by four separate publishers, each appearance prompting a lawsuit by my publisher. For ghost words, that's like a bestseller.

*Borges might argue that* diffiction *and* nonfiction *are actually the same thing. I remember "Ulrikke" says something like, "My story will be faithful to reality, or at least to my personal recollection of reality, which is the same thing."*

Then again, maybe Borges wouldn't. Another story I've always loved is "The Other Duel": my favorite line from that story goes, "I set these memories down here for what they are worth and with no further assurances as to their veracity, since both forgetfulness and recollection are creative."

A word related to *diffiction* is *bifiction*. My chapbook *At a Loss* was almost dropped a month before its publication: the publisher was having difficulty marketing it. Reviewers were confused, said *At a Loss* seemed to be "somehow both fiction and nonfiction, all at once." I later used those reviews to write *bifiction*, which I defined as "a work that contains both sections that are intentionally fictional and sections that are intentionally nonfictional."

*Why would you bother to invent new labels, if the labels we already have are "restricting"?*

I guess the categories do seem useful to me, at least as a system of organization. Even if nothing is ever totally fictional or totally nonfictional, I do like being able to divvy things up into different groups. If I have a name for something, then I understand it, and there's no reason for me to be afraid of it. It's only the nameless things that frighten me.

Like this interview. If these things I was saying were anonymous, just stapled to utility poles, they might seem scary, seem like some sort of threat. But when you attach "Michael Martone" to them, then everyone thinks, ah, okay, it's just that troublemaker from Fort Wayne.

Or like how an act of violence will become seemingly understandable once we're able to attach a name to it. When someone finds a body in a field, there's this terror in the community. But when the police release the name of the killer—just a suspect, even, a John Smith—in the community there's this widespread feeling of relief. *Even if the suspect hasn't yet been caught.* Because it's not a senseless crime anymore. John Smith did it—that we can understand. It's why we name our hurricanes.

# AN INTERVIEW WITH MICHAEL MARTONE

Depending on whom you ask, Michael Martone is either contemporary literature's most notorious prankster, innovator, or mutineer. In 1985 his AAP membership was briefly revoked after Martone published his first two books—a "prose" collection titled *Alive and Dead in Indiana* and a "poetry" collection titled *Return to Powers*—which, aside from *Return to Powers*' line breaks, were word-for-word identical. His membership to the Fellowship of English Writers was revoked in 1999 after FEW discovered that, while Martone's registered nom de plume had been "born" in the town of Reading, Martone himself never even had been to England. His AWP membership was revoked in 2007, reinstated in 2008, and revoked again in 2010.

After his first two books, Martone went on to write *Michael Martone*, a collection of fictional contributor's notes originally published among nonfictional contributor's notes in cooperative journals; *The Blue Guide to Indiana*, a collection of travel articles reviewing fictional attractions such as the Basilica di Jeff Gordon and the memorial to the Evansville Casserole Boycott of 1992 (most of which were, again, originally published as nonfiction); fictional interviews with his mentor Robert Coover; fictional advertisements in the margins of magazines such as *Glimmer Train* and *Electric Literature*; poems under the names of nonfictional colleagues; and blurbs for nonexistent books.

But his latest book is perhaps the most revealing: *Racing in Place* is a collection of essays exploring his obsession with name-brand clothing, sponsored tattooing, and human billboards, symbols of "America's meteoric plummet into the trudian age." Born in Fort Wayne, Indiana, Martone is often described as a nationalist, and his relationship with the United States mirrors his relationship with literature: he thinks of the United States as "a country in which local identities are being obliterated by corporate ones."

Martone now lives in Tuscaloosa, where he teaches in the MFA program at the University of Alabama. For our interview we agreed to meet at Tuscaloosa's Odette Odile Tavern, founded in 1819, the same year as its state. Martone wrote he would be "the one wearing a gray ascot and deerstalker cap." When I arrived at the tavern, three separate men (sitting alone at separate tables) were wearing gray ascots and deerstalker caps. I later learned Martone had hired two professors from the university's theater department to pose as "alternate" Martones. I approached the actual Martone (in preparing for the interview, I had spent most of the past month with his books, each of which is emblazoned with an author's photo circa 1981) and introduced myself, at which point the other Martones stood, tipped their caps, and left.

After the interview, Martone told me that it wouldn't have mattered which Martone I chose anyway. "Whichever one you sat down with was going to answer your questions."

*When did you decide you wanted to be a writer?*

In fourth grade I went to the Michigan state finals for the McDonald's When I Grow Up Speech Competition. My speech was about how I wanted to be Roald Dahl. So I must have decided sometime before fourth grade, although I'm not sure exactly when.

*How did you end up in the Michigan state finals? I thought you grew up in Fort Wayne.*

I did, but there was an incident in third grade, as a result of which I had to take a year off from the public school system in Indiana. So my mom sent me to live with my uncle in Michigan.

*Does "had to take a year off" mean "was expelled"?*

Well, yes. But I wasn't really *deviant*. I was just *unlucky*.

40

...

Okay, look, what happened was—I was in love, totally moonstruck, with this girl Mary Toft, and my friend Paul French was always trying to get me to prank call her, and so one day we did. We called her, and I was on the phone in my bedroom and Paul was on the phone in my kitchen, and when Mary answered we said something like, "We kidnapped your dog, and unless you give us twenty dollars and two of your school pictures, we're doing to drown her in your swimming pool a week from tonight." Which when you're in third grade means, translated: "I think you're cute." Mary thought the whole thing was sort of dumb, kept saying, "You don't have my dog, you idiot, I'm looking at her right now," but we kept saying, "No, that's not your dog, that's just a fake."

Then we hung up. But what we didn't know is that Mary hadn't been the only one on the line at her house: her dad had picked up another phone. And he was furious. He called our number back—this was before caller ID, when you had to dial *69 to trace a number—and I picked up the bedroom phone and Paul picked up the kitchen phone and Mary's dad was on the other end shouting questions. "Who the hell is this? What the hell do you want? What are you freaks doing calling my daughter?" We gave him fake names, of course. He wanted to talk to my parents, but I said, "My mom's not home," and hung up the phone.

But what we didn't know is that we—Paul and I—hadn't been the only ones on the line at *my* house. When Mary's dad called us back, my mom had heard the ringing phones and had picked up the phone in the basement and had heard everything.

So then she came upstairs and hit me with a wooden ladle for a while, in front of Paul, who I remember thought this was all sort of funny, and then she sent Paul home. Paul wasn't allowed back for a month, and I had to go to Mary's house and deliver a handwritten apology *in person* to Mary's dad. It was mortifying.

*You were expelled over that?*

No, that should have been the end of it. And for the next few months it was. But later that spring Paul and I invented this game involving cologne. Paul had an older brother, nicknamed "Stols," who had a ponytail and a leather jacket and was always going out on dates with mathletes and debaters. Anyway, the game was, whenever Stols was getting ready for a date, we would swipe a bottle of cologne from his dresser and sneak up behind him and squirt him. Then he would throw something at us or punch us and then we'd run away and hide. Then, later, we'd sneak back out and squirt him again. The result was, by the time he left to pick up his date, he would reek of this cologne. The cologne wasn't bad, but it wasn't meant to be worn in thirteen-squirt doses. That concentrated, it smelled like cologne you'd get at a convenience store.

Anyway, after a while, squirting Stols wasn't enough anymore. The game was a drug, and we had developed a tolerance. No matter how many times we'd squirt him, we couldn't get that buzz that we remembered, that "fun" high. So we decided to take the cologne to school.

Most of the day we just squirted kids walking around in the hall. Paul would squirt someone in the back, then pocket the bottle. Whoever we squirted would smell for the rest of the day but wouldn't know why. We thought this was hugely funny.

Then Paul decided what would be *really* funny would be if we dumped the rest of the bottle on a single person. Again, we had developed a tolerance. We had to up the stakes.

So after lunch Paul took off the cap and handed me the bottle and then as we were walking down the hall we saw our friend Robby Todino coming and Paul started tapping me with his hand which meant *him him him* and so when Robby got closer I jerked the bottle at him, but Robby saw, and ducked, and the cologne hit Mary Toft instead, who had been walking behind him. Half a bottle of cologne. Which, again, wouldn't have been that big of a deal, except that Mary turned out to have a severe allergy to fragrances.

*You hadn't known about that beforehand?*

No! We had no idea. All I knew about her was that she had gray eyes and a cute nose. How was I supposed to know her throat closed and her skin blistered anytime she got within a hundred yards of aftershave? And, anyway, I had been aiming at somebody else entirely.

But after that her dad really came after us: he said the incident had been "an attempt on her life," and he brought in pictures of these hideous rashes that had broken out on her skin, and even still everything might have been okay, except he also said that I had been "making threats" and brought in my handwritten apology note as evidence.

So then I was expelled.

But that year in Michigan ended up being pivotal for me. Michigan has a history of nurturing artists: Fregoli, Hemingway, Frostic, Madonna. Even though I was the new kid, I became the class star when I started winning those speech competitions: our class competition, then the district, then the city, then the region, all the way to state. I ended up losing at state, though, to some kid from Midland. He claimed he wanted to be an astronaut. His speech wasn't any good, but the judges couldn't not vote for a "future American hero." This kid even wore one of those collared shirts that look like a flag—red and white stripes, with stars across one sleeve.

I was so bitter about losing that I've kept tabs on that kid ever since. I may not have won the competition, but I have become what I set out to be—the astronaut kid, now, just works at some office building in Rhode Island. His company makes paper clips.

*Once you had decided you wanted to be a writer, how did you go about actually becoming one?*

Well, I wrote stories. In sixth grade I wrote a book about a chameleon named Gege who lives on an island and has to go off on some quest. In ninth grade I wrote a book about a ghost named Tom who meets a shadow and has to go off on some quest. In twelfth grade I wrote a book about a scarecrow named Piper who adopts this orphan and, of course, has to go off on some quest.

Even then, though, I knew these things I was writing were derivative of other writers I loved: Lois Lowry, Roald Dahl, Madeleine L'Engle. Anytime I tried to write something, even if I *consciously avoided imitating them*, inevitably the story would turn into one of theirs.

So what I finally decided to do was this: I would go somewhere where nobody knew me, and I would create a fictional life. This, I thought, would be my education in storytelling. I would create an alternate identity. For a year of my life, every moment would be a fiction.

*When was this?*

After high school. I took a year off before college and moved to Cleveland.

*What did you name your alter ego?*

I can't tell you that. I've never told anyone that, not even my wife.

We can call him John Smith, if you want. But that's not his real name.

*You're usually forthcoming about your "experiments": why be so coy about your alter ego?*

I guess I'm afraid of being found by the people I knew that year. If those people became part of my life again, I would be forced to merge these two identities: Michael Martone and John Smith. Now, I'm able to keep those identities separate. Having to try to mix Martone and Smith into one coherent identity, that would be awful, truly awful, just wouldn't work.

*Did creating this fictional self actually teach you anything about writing?*

It taught me everything. It was my boot camp. If I had never trained myself in that way, I'd still be writing those knockoffs of Roald Dahl.

*But isn't writing a novel, or a short story, even, considerably more complicated than what you were doing? You were authoring a single character, "John Smith," while a story requires you to invent an entire cast of them, and a world for them to inhabit.*

What I was doing was *exactly* that complicated. I invented John Smith, but doing so required me to invent an entire history. I wasn't just attaching Michael Martone's story to a new name: I had to invent John Smith's grandparents, ex-lovers, former coworkers, fifth grade teachers. I had to invent anecdotes from his past: his first fistfight, the night his dog had puppies, his stepmother's suicide. I had to invent the landscape of his hometown: he'd grown up near the Titan Tower, in Utah, where I had never even been. I had to invent his future: he hoped to visit the ruins of a certain cabin, in Neal, Kansas, where his grandfather had been born; he dreamed of becoming a designer of board games; he knew someday he would have to scatter his uncle's ashes in Bowers, Indiana, near a certain sundial, to fulfill his uncle's wishes.

I had to be constantly focused, my tongue always ready to write. Even out just relaxing at some bar, like this, John Smith's friends might ask me suddenly, "Have you ever broken a bone?" Of course, as Michael Martone pretending to be John Smith, the easiest answer would be, "No." But I wasn't trying to write an *easy* fiction: I was trying to write a *compelling* fiction, a fiction these people in Cleveland would want to keep reading. So I'd say, "Yes, thirteen bones—a wrist, a leg, and about half of my ribs." And that would prompt other questions, and I'd have to keep filling the details in: how I'd broken my ribs, whose roof I'd fallen off of when I had broken my wrist, what color cast I'd had on my leg.

And that's what was so fun. Every day I got to learn more about John Smith, come closer to *who he really was*. Some of the details I learned were haunting. He had been through awful things—much more than I ever had. By the end, I really had come to love him.

*That "writing process" required other people, though: the friends, asking questions.*

Well, you can ask the questions yourself.

There's a graphic novelist who writes under the name Moebius. He's French, but he designed props for a number of American films: *Alien*, *The Abyss*, *Masters of the Universe*. His artwork inspired the set for *Blade Runner*, and the design of the probe droid in *Star Wars*.

My favorite graphic novel by Moebius is *The Airtight Garage*. For that novel, Moebius invented an unusual writing process. He was publishing the book serially, two pages per month, in *Métal Hurlant*. Fiction writers, like Dickens, used to be able to do write serial novels. Now magazines don't want serial novels, only standalone short stories.

Anyway, Moebius's process was this: in every installment he wrote, he would try to do two things. First, he would answer all of the questions raised by previous installments. Second, he would "dig [himself] into a hole he could not get out of"—in other words, add things to the story that contradicted previous installments, or that were seemingly impossible to explain. Things he had no *idea* how to connect to the overriding narrative.

Then, the next installment, he would start over, and have to answer all of the questions.

The result was astonishing. *The Airtight Garage* is only a hundred pages, but includes a huge cast of characters, and creates not just one *but several worlds in their entirety*. And even Moebius himself didn't know where the story was going, so as a reader there's simply no way to anticipate the turns in the plot. It's incredibly compelling.

*So is that where you recommend your students begin? Away from home, with an alter ego? A John Smith?*

Actually, I tell my students to start at an amusement park.

*Amusement park?*

At a Disneyland, specifically. Disneyland Paris, Shanghai Disneyland, Tokyo Disneyland, whichever. Anything Disney.

*What are your students supposed to learn there?*

In terms of profits, Disney's parks obliterate other amusement parks. In terms of annual visitors, the top seven amusement parks, worldwide, are all Disney. But why? Six Flags, in California; Cedar Point, in Ohio; Kings Dominion, in Virginia; those parks, they each have triple the roller coasters of any Disneyland. Triple the thrill. So, why, then? What's Disney's trick?

I'll tell you. The trick is that, at Disney's parks, a roller coaster *is never just a roller coaster*. The thrill *is never just a thrill*. Every ride comes with a narrative: the ride actually begins *while you're waiting in line*, because that's where the story, at Disney's parks, always begins. Splash Mountain isn't just dropping into some water from high above: you're part of Br'er Rabbit's narrative, actually dropping *from the climax of the story* into the resolution below. The Haunted Mansion, in its closing section, becomes second person, actually *adding you to the story* through the use of mirrors. Pirates of the Caribbean—which was the inspiration for the films, not vice versa—has a number of separate scenes, with a vast range of characters, each character exhibiting some desire, or conflict, *some intricate life*.

At those other parks, you're just flying around—experiencing a thrill, definitely, maybe a buzz, panic, fear—but in a narrative vacuum.

*Are you sponsored by Disney?*

I'm not sponsored by Disney. But I've learned from Disney. That's where any student of writing should begin. In line for the Carousel of Progress.

*You've endorsed other unusual methods of "training." I read that in your mid-fifties you spent a year living in a warehouse, alone, as an "anti-artist." What's an "anti-artist"? Someone opposed to art?*

No. And I wasn't alone. And I wasn't there "as an 'anti-artist.'" I was there studying the collective of anti-artists who squat in the warehouse.

*This was in Alabama?*

I can't say where the warehouse is, because the anti-artists are still there, and require secrecy.

*How did you find it?*

I can't say.

*What's an anti-artist?*

Here's the basic idea: There's an anti-artist there named Cavoye, this stooped trembly woman, who's blind, and who spends all day painting. There's an anti-artist there named Dauger, this squinty refugee, who's deaf, and who spends all day writing songs on a wooden harp. There's an anti-artist there named Eustache, this kid, who's mute, and who's supposedly illiterate in all languages, and who spends all day pounding out poems on an antique typewriter.

The idea is to produce art over which you have truly no control.

*Who organized this?*

I can't say.

*Do the anti-artists ever leave the warehouse?*

Really, I can't say any more.

*In your essay "Reincarnations: The Sextuple Stellar System of Mizar and Alcor" you said that you don't like being identified as a "poetry" or "prose" writer, that you find labels like those "restricting."*

I said that? I probably did, although doesn't "restricting" seem kind of extreme? I don't see those labels as being "restricting" so much as "superfluous"—unable to create any meaningful distinction. The first story I ever sold was a poem called "The Horn Papers." I hadn't been able to sell it as a poem, so I just took out the line breaks and submitted it as prose.

*You later did that on a larger scale with* Alive and Dead in Indiana *and* Return to Powers. *How does that make those labels "superfluous," though?*

It's like hot dogs.

*Like what?*

If you took those leftover meat products often sold in tube form under the name "hot dog"—the kidneys of pigs, the hearts of cattle—and packaged them in some other form instead—donut form, for example, or in the shape of a pretzel—would anyone buy them?

*…?*

Something about the form of a hot dog reassures the American public. Eating a slush of meat and preservatives, if packaged in tube form, is desirable. If packaged in can form, however, with a picture of a cat on the side of the can, eating that same slush then becomes undesirable.

Which brings us to the first rule of both capitalism and art: the form must fit the content. The second rule is implied: if the form is changed, the content must change. If you expect anyone to eat it, that is. "It" being your product, your art.

For me, the problem was that flash fiction evolved out of the prose gene pool, and prose poetry evolved out of the poetry gene pool, and they seemed like basically the same thing. If I were to witness a prose poem holding up a convenience store, and if that prose poem were later herded into a police lineup along with nine innocent flash fictions, I can already tell you that I wouldn't be able to pick out the prose poem: I'd start sweating, wringing my hands, eventually have to admit that maybe I didn't get that good of a look at the poem with the gun after all.

Which was a problem because I had been under the impression that poetry and prose were mutually exclusive categories. I thought, either something is prose and not poetry, or something is poetry and not prose.

But now something could be prose *and* poetry. Which seemed to suggest that a novel could be poetry, or that a sonnet could be prose. And if "poetry" and "prose" were no longer capable of differentiating between distinct forms of writing, then to me they no longer seemed worth maintaining.

Others get confused by this, too. Have you read Carsten René Nielsen, that Danish poet? A few years ago Nielsen published a collection of prose poems called *House Inspections*. *The Paris Review* published ten of the poems from *House Inspections* in their No. 191 issue—except that someone at *The Paris Review* must have mistranslated something, because in the magazine the poems appeared under the category of "fiction." Right alongside Aimee Bender and Patricio Pron—as if Nielsen were a writer of prose, a writer of flash fictions.

And maybe he is. Maybe what he writes *is* more prose than poetry. But he considers himself a poet. His website announced *The Paris Review* had published ten of his "poems."

*Do these two "rules" apply only to writing, or art in general?*

Anything. Film, sculpture, gymnastics. Maurice Sendak, for example, wrote by the first rule: *Where the Wild Things Are* succeeds because the content, the story, was perfectly tailored to its form, the picture book. Spike Jonze's adaptation also succeeds, but only because his film follows the second rule: because he was working in a different form, he was forced to alter the content—expanding the story, naming unnamed characters, inventing new characters, writing new scenes—so that *Where the Wild Things Are* would have the right waist to support its new pants, the right shoulders to fill out its new shirt. Those same alterations were necessary when converting the graphic novels *American Splendor* and *Ghost World* to film: they both succeed in their new form, but only because their content has been drastically changed.

Of course, when changing the form of a work of art, it isn't enough simply to alter the content: the content must be altered *well*. Instead, more often than not, the content is altered in a clumsy, sloppy way, by someone indifferent to—or even completely unfamiliar with—the original content. Films based on video games are especially notorious for this: *Super Mario Bros.*, *Tomb Raider*, *Street Fighter*, *Double Dragon*, they're some of the worst films ever made. Online, *Super Mario Bros.* has an average rating of 3.1. *3.1 out of 10.*

These rules apply not only to different mediums of storytelling, but to forms within the mediums themselves. Take a work of prose, for example: David Foster Wallace packaged "Incarnations of Burned Children" in the form of flash fiction. If he had tried to package it in a different prose form—the short story, the novella, the novel—it would have failed. For his story to succeed as a novel, it would have to become a different story altogether.

*So when you're writing, how do you decide whether to package something as poetry or prose?*

When choosing the form for your content, you should be aware that every form has certain capabilities unique to that form alone. And, at the same time, certain incapabilities. So what can poetry do that prose can't? Well, prose writers have limited control over the rhythm of their writing, and its visual appearance. The only tools a prose writer even has for that are punctuation—periods, commas, ellipses, colons—and paragraph, section, and chapter breaks.

A poet's toolbox, however, is stocked with all sorts of these tools. Poetry isn't bound by the same rules that prose is, or any rules. Poets can use line breaks wherever, indent whatever they'd like however they'd like, throw whole pages of white space between one line and the next. Plus, poetry comes with a number of helpful forms—the ghazal, the cinquain, the jintishi, the villanelle—that have already been discovered to have certain rhythmic and visual qualities.

*So when writing prose poems, poets are essentially locking themselves out of their toolbox—forcing themselves to produce a poem with only the limited tools given to a writer of prose.*

To me, poetry's capabilities seem best suited for aesthetic writing. Aesthetic, here, meaning "chiefly interested in producing an aural or visual effect." Walt Whitman's poems, for example, seem meant to act as symphonies, to use certain linguistic melodies to charm the reader, to draw the reader into a trance. Or E. E. Cummings's poems, those often act as paintings, these unreadable tapestries of numerals, punctuation marks, fragments of language.

Prose has its own capabilities, but doesn't lend itself to manipulating aesthetics so much as manipulating narrative. David Foster Wallace used footnotes, mathematical symbols, parenthetical asides to produce narrative effects that would be impossible to achieve anywhere other than the written page. Even when simply reading his stories out loud—adapting them from written stories to oral stories—some aspect of them is lost.

I'm sometimes tempted to suggest the terms "poetry" and "prose" be replaced by "aesthetics" and "narratives." Anyway, when I'm writing, here's how I decide: if I'm trying to use language to do the work of a storyteller, I use prose; if I'm trying to use language to do the work of a composer or a painter, I use poetry.

Or, like *Larus* seagulls.

*Seagulls?*

Typically how you can differentiate between different species is by breeding: if two organisms can interbreed and produce fertile offspring, they're the same species; if they can't, they aren't.

But here's the odd thing about *Larus* seagulls. These birds form a ring around the Arctic, from northern Canada to northern Russia to northern Scandinavia to northern Britain and back across the ocean to northern Canada. And if you take one of the birds from Canada, and if you take one of the birds from Scandinavia, they can't interbreed. They're completely different seagulls—so different they can't even reproduce.

But, at some point along the continuum, the Canadian gulls and the Scandinavian gulls *become the same bird.* They merge, they interbreed, they give birth to mutt gulls that are a mix of both species, of their Canadian and their Scandinavian genes.

So I don't worry anymore, that poetry and prose were supposed to be these distinct species but have become so similar at one point along the continuum that they can interbreed. I don't worry anymore, because I have a name for it. Now I think of them as a ring species, like the gulls: different species, but also one.

*"Poetry" and "prose" may be problematic terms, but wouldn't "aesthetics" and "narratives" be just as problematic?*

At the very least we need a new name for poetry. Just as a matter of marketing. In the same way that "comics" once was dismissed as a medium for children, was relegated to producing juvenile stories for a limited and highly ridiculed audience, but then was reinvented by Will Eisner as the "graphic novel," and has since become a medium for adults, a medium with a growing and highly esteemed audience—couldn't "poetry," too, be reinvented? In a genius marketing scheme, couldn't American consumers be fooled by a new brand name for what's seen as an outdated product? Couldn't poets sell, finally, some books? Actually make a living from their work? If Americans have been taught to dismiss poetry as something for "geeks," or "queers," or "snobs," couldn't we rebrand it—whether we called it "aesthetics," or "page songs," or "naked novels," or "baroque vogue collectable wordworks"—as something hip, as something trendy, as the very latest thing? Isn't it really, after all, that easy to manipulate American consumers?

*Does your work as a poet ever inform your work as a writer of prose? Or vice versa?*

I was writing a new story, recently, called "Two Noble Kinsmen." The story has six sections, which alternate between the perspectives of three different characters. And, as I was writing the story, I began thinking about each section as a very enormous line. I decided to set up a rhyme scheme, ABCCBA, for the six sections, repeating the final words. So the first and ultimate sections end with "doing," the second and penultimate sections end with "body," and the middle sections both end with "light." That scheme forced me to take the story in directions I wouldn't have otherwise, similar to how the content of a ghazal or a jintishi is often steered by its form.

In that sense "Two Noble Kinsmen" might be considered both poetry and prose. It's essentially narrative, but also was written with the intent of producing certain aesthetic effects. If you want to call it a story, I'll let you. If you want to call it a poem, I'll let you. I've packaged this particular blend of meat and preservatives, and I don't care what you call it, as long as you eat it, and enjoy it, and come away full.

*In your essay "The Voynich Manuscript, the* Codex Seraphinianus, *and the Corrupted Blood Incident of Zul'Gurub," you mentioned you own a Kindle. What are you feelings on print versus ebook? Is print doomed?*

Depends on the publishers. If print is going to survive, someone is going to have to start printing books that are more than just cheap paper and a shiny cover. If you can pay $7 for an ebook edition of *Infinite Jest* that weighs zero ounces or $13 for a print edition of *Infinite Jest* that weighs three pounds, and if they're *exactly the same book*, who's going to pay more money for a bulkier version? Ebooks are cheaper to publish, quicker to distribute, and easier to carry. My generation grew up with print only, so we have a certain nostalgia that may keep print around another few decades. Your generation grew up between, so I imagine your loyalties will lie between, too. But this next generation—the kids who have grown up with touchscreens and the internet and have never known anything different—they'll be the ones to bury print.

I do think print could survive. But for that to happen, publishers need to start thinking about the book as an *object*: books will have to become so extraordinary, visually and tactilely, that consumers will want to own the *thing*, regardless of whether they actually want to read it. Bookmaking will have to become an art form again, rather than simply a process of mass production.

My mother bought this 1950s crank-powered eggbeater recently, for example. She already has an electronic hand mixer and a state-of-the-art blender: there's nothing she can do with this eggbeater that she wasn't already able to do faster and easier with those other tools. But when she saw this eggbeater, at an antique store in the Carolinas, she was so struck by the design—the polished wood of its handle, the engravings along its metal cogs—that she bought it anyway. And now she uses that instead of her hand mixer. It's slower, it's harder, but it's so appealing as an object that she's willing to put in that extra work, just to have her hands on it, to become a part of that design. The hand mixer she keeps in a cupboard. The eggbeater she hangs from a knob over her oven, keeping it on display.

That's what books need to become. Publishers need to give consumers a reason to want the object: blueprint pages, litmus pages, parchment pages, illustrations that unfold like accordions, chapbooks bound with twigs. That's why *McSweeney's* is so popular: the actual content of *McSweeney's* isn't any better than the average literary quarterly's, but each issue of *McSweeney's* is a remarkable object, somehow unique. I'm happy to read issues of *The New Yorker* online, but *McSweeney's* I want to be able to touch, to examine, to will to my children.

*So it's all up to the publishers? There's nothing writers can do to save print?*

Well, if print's to survive, writers need to find *reasons* to have their books printed—need to start using storytelling techniques that can only be achieved on the printed page. Salvador Plascencia does this, for example, in *The People of Paper*: at one point in the novel there's a die cut, where a character's name has been actually snipped from the page. In an ebook, sure, you could whiteout the name, or cover it with a black rectangle—but those techniques are used in the book too, and they serve a different purpose. The die cut is performing a specific task. And you can't create an actual hole in an ebook.

*Do you consider your "sticker fiction" a form of print?*

Do you mean Dean Strickland? Dean Strickland isn't my only sticker fiction. The sticker fictions actually started with my Pulitzer project.

You know how after a book wins the Pulitzer Prize, the publisher will mail out those gold stickers that say WINNER OF THE PULITZER PRIZE for libraries to slap onto the covers of all of their copies? Go to your library and find a copy of *A Visit from the Goon Squad* that was published before 2011, or a copy of *The Brief Wondrous Life of Oscar Wao* that was published before 2008—they'll have the gold sticker. Anyway, I started making my own WINNER OF THE PULITZER PRIZE stickers. I found a company in Tuscaloosa that would print them for me in batches of a thousand. Then whenever I went somewhere to give a reading, I would stop in at a couple libraries and put the stickers on books that never won. I started with *The Man in the High Castle*, and after that Barry's *One Hundred Demons*, and after that Guest's *Symbiosis*. Then I switched to the Nobel: I awarded that to *Labyrinths*, and different issues of *The Sandman*.

*How did you decide which books to "award"?*

My criterion: anything that deserved recognition that didn't stand a chance in hell of getting it. Borges, he was always troubled that he had never won the Nobel Prize—awarding *Labyrinths* was my tribute to him. I was giving him what he should have won. I don't work for the Nobel Foundation, of course, so my award was a sort of fiction. But Borges adored fictions—part of me suspects he would value that fictional prize even more than the nonfictional.

Anyway, it was that project that inspired my sons to invent Dean Strickland the Hitchhiking Guitarman. We made bumper stickers with his silhouette—my silhouette, plus a cowboy hat—and his name. Now whenever we're visiting somewhere, we pop them onto the backs of stop signs, the sides of dumpsters, et cetera. If you peek into that bathroom over there, there's one on the mirror.

*Any other new projects?*

I've been writing neologisms for Urban Dictionary. *Nom* was one of my words. *Ugshot, orly, geekquinox*. I've also been developing fictional characters for Facebook and Twitter. Dean is on Facebook, now, and Twitter too. I maintain dozens of characters on those sites, though, so keeping up can be difficult. "Wisdom is like turtle soup, in that not everybody can get it."

*Have you been doing any other "work" online?*

No, that's it.

*Honestly?*

Yes, honestly.

*In an interview with* Granta *you alluded to having enlisted with the hacktivist group Anonymous.*

You can't "enlist" with Anonymous. Anonymous has no hierarchy, no protocols, no ceremonies whatsoever. There are no leaders. Membership is instantaneous: by wishing to join, you've joined. Resigning is instantaneous: by wishing to quit, you've quit.
  Ask me if I belong to Anonymous.

*Do you belong to Anonymous?*

Yes. Ask me again.

*Do you belong to Anonymous?*

No. Ask me again.

*Do you belong to Anonymous?*

Both answers were true. *That is not a contradiction.* Between answers, the truth changed.

*But, usually, you belong to Anonymous?*

Here's what won't ever change: like Anonymous, I am anti-censorship, anti-propaganda, anti-tyranny, anti-military, anti-cartel, anti-cult, anti-sexism, anti-racism, anti-sizism, anti-hate. I am for Julian Assange, and Aidan Delgado, and Camilo Mejía, and Josh Key. I have always been, and am, and always will be, against Guantanamo Bay. I have seen Orihime Inoue spin a leek.

*But you can write code?*

Sudo.

*"Psuedo"?*

And isn't there something beautiful, *something miraculous*, about white hats, gray hats, black hats, these wizards of coding, somehow putting aside their differences, and gathering their electric wands, and coming together to battle American monsters like Fred Phelps?

*But who decides who the monster is?*

Anonymous decides.

*By, what, voting?*

Within Anonymous, thought is collective. There truly is no identity. The ego is undone, dismissed. Names are thrown out, pseudonyms taken up. I didn't say, "The members of Anonymous decide." I said, "Anonymous decides." Which of your brain cells decides what you'll do next? There is no which. It's your brain.
So, no, the hackers don't vote. Anonymous is a multiorganism consciousness. "Multiorganism" isn't a word, officially, because there's never been a multiorganism anything before. But, here, that's the only word for it.

*Who do you see as your influences?*

FM-2030, obviously. Princess Caraboo. Bruegel's *Children's Games*, *The Tower of Babel*, *The Blind Leading the Blind*. I've also always admired Haruki Murakami, especially *Hard-Boiled Wonderland and the End of the World*. I'd like to spend an afternoon as Murakami, experiencing everyday life as filtered through his brain. He's the personification of the American short story—experiences reality through metaphor. "The doors of all the world's refrigerators seemed to have been thrown open at once." "Silence descended and began to burrow its way into the folds of my brain, one after another, like an insect laying eggs." "Still, I felt the presence of something here that was trying to deceive me, as if the others were holding their breath, pressing themselves flat against the wall, obliterating their skin color to keep me from knowing they were there. So I pretended not to notice. We were very good at fooling each other."

*Paul Gravett claims Murakami was profoundly influenced by manga, in the same way that I've read you were influenced by comics. Murakami said, "For me, the manga Maki Sasaki drew have had the continued effect of opening a window to a particular place inside me. Through my books, I wanted to pass onto the younger generation that same intensity which Sasaki provided for my generation." Are there any artists in particular that opened that window for you?*

That year that I was living in Cleveland as "John Smith," I briefly fell in with Harvey Pekar and R. Crumb. Pekar was still working on early drafts of what would become the first issue of *American Splendor*—Crumb, too, was still largely unknown. Pekar really didn't like Smith, but Crumb thought Smith was okay. We were into collecting LPs. We'd hang out at Pekar's apartment, listening to *The Rise and Fall of Ziggy Stardust and the Spiders from Mars*, to soundtracks from the Man With No Name trilogy. And we'd read comics.

Before that I hadn't had any interest in comics. In the 1950s Fredric Wertham had published *Seduction of the Innocent*, a homophobic "psychology" book about comics that started a national witch-hunting movement and eventually led to the founding of the CCA: the Comics Code Authority, although the acronym just as easily could have stood for the Comics Censorship Authority. The CCA had a rating system with a single stamp: either it was approved or it wasn't.

*What determined whether a comic was approved by the CCA?*

The CCA had a list of General Standards: "No unique or unusual methods of concealing weapons shall be shown"; "Policemen, judges, government officials and respected institutions shall never be presented in such a way as to create disrespect for established authority"; "All characters shall be depicted in dress reasonably acceptable to society"; et cetera.

The effect of Wertham's witch-hunting would have been less obvious with nonserial literature. When *The Grapes of Wrath* was banned, for example, there weren't any obvious effects within the world of literature, aside from *The Grapes of Wrath* getting removed from a number of libraries and being read by just about everyone. But when one week Clark Kent could say, "G'morning Lois! Toss me one of them donuts, willya?" and the next week he was required to say instead, "Good morning, Lois! Will you hand me a donut?"—another General Standard was that "wherever possible good grammar shall be employed"—the effects were fairly obvious.

Before this, comics had been a medium for gritty, adult stories. But the CCA's rules sank the enormously successful EC Comics, known for their horror titles, within a year. The CCA was devastating for American comics. European comics, the bandes dessinées, continued to mature, and flourish, and evolve. Japanese comics, manga, became their storytelling forte, their leading cultural export. It was only in America that comics became a medium for "children," and only because our comics were being censored.

But in the '70s artists like Pekar and Crumb revived the medium. Their comics rejected the superhero genre: they wanted to write about real life, about people they knew from the streets of Cleveland. Meanwhile, there I was, as John Smith, living among them with an alter ego. My project fused the superhero story with their stories—real-life Cleveland, but still a man with a mask.

*What attracts you to those kinds of projects? Your Cleveland alter ego, your internet alter egos?*

It's a sort of playing. Similar, I guess, to those games Paul and I used to play. The literary equivalent of prank calling. When I was in Cleveland talking to Crumb, he thought he was only talking to John Smith: he never realized someone else was on the line, listening in.

*But those games got you into trouble.*

That's the artist's job, to test those rules, to take those risks, to play those sorts of games. If we allow a literary CCA to tell us what's "permissible" as literature, what fiction is or isn't, what nonfiction is or isn't, what's poetry or not poetry or what's prose or not prose, it will limit the art we're capable of making. I'm not saying my fictions have been groundbreaking or successful or even all that original. But they have challenged the conventional model for what fiction can be.

*So it's more than prank calling?*

I see myself as more than just a performance artist. My fictions are meant to be more than funny, do more than make a point. I try to find something human in them. And I don't know if they've ever reached anyone else. But my own life has been the better for them.

# AN INTERVIEW WITH MICHAEL MARTONE

Depending on whom you ask, Michael Martone is either contemporary literature's most notorious prankster, innovator, or mutineer. In 1985 his AAP membership was briefly revoked after Martone published his first two books—a "prose" collection titled *Alive and Dead in Indiana* and a "poetry" collection titled *The Flatness and Other Landscapes*—which, aside from *The Flatness and Other Landscapes*' line breaks, were word-for-word identical. His membership to the Society of Scottish Novelists was revoked in 1999 after SSN discovered that, while Martone's registered nom de plume had been "born" on the Isle of Skye, Martone himself never even had been to Scotland. His AWP membership was revoked in 2007, reinstated in 2008, and revoked again in 2010.

After his first two books, Martone went on to write *Michael Martone*, a collection of fictional contributor's notes originally published among nonfictional contributor's notes in cooperative journals; *The Blue Guide to Indiana*, a collection of travel articles reviewing fictional attractions such as the Pieta de Styrofoam and a monument to the Fallen Grocers of the 1983 Walmart Invasion (most of which were, again, originally published as nonfiction); fictional interviews with his mentor Thomas Pynchon; fictional advertisements in the margins of magazines such as *Narrative* and *BOMB*; poems using the names of nonfictional colleagues; and blurbs for nonexistent books.

But his latest book is perhaps the most revealing: *Racing in Place* is a collection of essays exploring his obsession with superheroes, mascots, and logos, symbols of "these cultural masks that invite mimicry." Born in Fort Wayne, Indiana, Martone is often described as an economist, and his financial convictions mirror his literary: he has labeled the copyright, for example, a "cultural aberration."

Martone and I met while sharing a taxi from the seven-star Burj Al Arab to Dubai International Airport. When I suggested Martone be interviewed, Martone agreed, but on the condition I pay for our taxi. This interview was conducted during the course of our ride.

*I've read that when you were younger you fought as an eco-terrorist, for several years, in the wilds of Venezuela.*

No. That anecdote—like most of the anecdotes you'll hear about me—simply isn't true. I did fight as an eco-terrorist, but it was the wilds of Indiana, not Venezuela. And it wasn't just when I was younger—I'm an eco-terrorist still. Although I should say that, when interviewing an eco-terrorist, you probably should be aware that the proper term is eco-soldier.

*I was surprised when I read that you had been, or were, an eco-soldier. Your work itself doesn't seem to have any political agenda.*

My fiction isn't work—my fiction is me at play. My work is what I do as an eco-soldier. But even that doesn't have a political agenda. If we do have an agenda, it's an ecological one.

My ecological work is with a group called AVALANCHE, which was founded by my friend Paul French. Have you read Paul's novel? Paul wrote a novel called *Planetarium*, which he self-published in a shed on his parents' farm just outside of Fort Wayne. Each page of *Planetarium* is nailed to the walls or the windows of this rickety toolshed. These pages aren't numbered—aren't ordered in any way. But they wallpaper the walls, plaster the windows, hang from the rafters. These are, incidentally, typewritten pages. When the sunlight hits the windows above the bench, you can't read those pages: they light up, shine bright white, their words disappear. And even today, *Planetarium* is still there. You can go to the farm, and if you ask Paul's parents about *Planetarium*, they'll take you out back, and leave you in the shed, and you can stay as long as you want, reading. "Who prevents you from inventing waterproof gunpowder?" My wife, in her mid-thirties, lived in the shed for almost a week, reading and rereading Paul's novel. Some of the pages are hidden—taped to the underside of the toolbox, tucked into the blades of the lawn mower, crumpled between the teeth of a pair of pliers—and my wife became obsessed with reading every page. Back then, she wasn't my wife—we hadn't even met yet. Paul's parents called him, after my wife had been living in his novel for about a week, and said, "We don't mind your readers coming to visit, Paul, but we're starting to think that this one's moved in for good." So Paul drove out to meet her. Eventually she joined AVALANCHE, which is how we met.

*How did the group get its name?*

Again, thanks to Paul. When he was a teenager, Paul was in a band, called AVALANCHE, that only covered songs by fictional bands. The band wasn't named AVALANCHE for any reason, really: fourteen-year-old Paul just loved the word. And, every group he's been in since, he's insisted on naming AVALANCHE. He started a reading series at Capgras College, in West Virginia, which he named Capgras College's AVALANCHE Visiting Writers Series. I have never understood how he gets people to go along with that sort of thing.

The band's songs are online, now, if you want to look them up. My favorite is "Telescopic," originally written by the fictional band Drugs for Droogs. Paul and his bandmates invented Drugs for Droogs, including a backstory—that they were was founded in LA in the '60s; that they had sworn eternal devotion to the fairy queen Titania; that they developed a cult following in the flatlands of Missouri; that their bassist and drummer were both killed in a train accident just weeks after "Telescopic" went gold—and then Paul and his bandmates wrote Drugs for Droogs' song "Telescopic" and covered the song on AVALANCHE's first album. Paul got ahold of some photos—he won't say whether the photos were of an actual band not named Drugs for Droogs, or whether he just hired these dreadlocked bodybuilders to pose as Drugs for Droogs—anyway, Paul got ahold of some photos of these guys standing on a rooftop, shirtless, holding guitars and drumsticks and et cetera, with this flock of pigeons taking off in the background, which Paul and his bandmates included in their liner notes, with a caption that read "Drugs for Droogs, 1963," along with photos of all of the other fictional bands.

*What's AVALANCHE's ecological agenda?*

The band AVALANCHE didn't have any ecological agenda—theirs was basically a get-cute-girls-to-fall-in-love-with-us agenda. The eco-soldier group AVALANCHE, however, has an ecological agenda that's complex and knotty and varies from region to region.

...

Well so I'll try. When I said our agenda was solely ecological, that may have been somewhat misleading. Because AVALANCHE is also anti-capitalist, in certain respects. Our country—you are an American, aren't you?—our country is a country in which local identities are being obliterated by corporate ones. Fort Wayne has been overrun by the chains. The chain restaurants. In Fort Wayne, you cannot eat at a restaurant that is locally owned anymore, a restaurant whose menu has been invented and designed by someone who actually lives in Fort Wayne. In Fort Wayne you can eat at Applebee's, O'Charley's, Chi-Chi's, Bennigan's, Logan's, Denny's. You can eat at Damon's Grill, which was not founded by someone named Damon, but was instead founded by people named Irv and Jerry and Sam and Joe, people who named it Damon's for marketing reasons. You can eat at Jason's Deli, which was not founded by someone named Jason, but instead by people named Joe and Rusty and Pete and Pat. There is no Damon. There is no Jason. Our locally owned restaurants, named for actual people, have been obliterated by corporate restaurants wearing the names of fictional ones.

And it's not just the restaurants. It's our hotels, our hardware stores, our cookware stores, our automobile repair shops. American cities have become every other American city. If you live in Fort Wayne, why bother to vacation in Myrtle Beach? Myrtle Beach is just a slightly warmer Fort Wayne. You'll eat at all of the same places. You'll shop at the same pharmacies. If you forgot your swimsuit in Fort Wayne, you can get the exact same swimsuit at the mall in Myrtle Beach. The same size, the same color, hanging from the exact same sort of hanger.

We've left the modern era, have finally entered the trudian age.

*"Trudian"?*

Trudian! "If on arriving at Trude I had not read the city's name in big letters, I would have thought I was landing at the same airport from which I had taken off. The suburbs they drove me through were no different from the others, with the same little greenish and yellowish houses. Following the same signs we swung around the same flower beds in the same squares. The downtown streets displayed goods, packages, signs that had not changed at all. This was the first time I had come to Trude, but I already knew the hotel where I happened to be lodged; I had already spoken my dialogues with the buyers and sellers of hardware; I had ended other days identically, looking through the same goblets at the same swaying navels. Why come to Trude? I asked myself. I already wanted to leave. 'Resume your flight whenever you like,' they said, 'but you will arrive at another Trude, absolutely the same, detail by detail. The land is covered by a sole Trude which does not begin and does not end. Only the name of the airport changes."

And when that's our landscape, as a people, that affects each and every one of us. You think there aren't other Michael Martones? You can go to any city in the US and find some man exactly like me: wearing the same clothes, eating the same hamburgers, napping on the same furniture, complaining about these same things. We have no uniqueness, anymore. We are people who wear different names despite that we are all the same person. What the chains have done on a corporate scale has happened to us on a personal. We are a nation of clones.

*But a restaurant being part of that chain, though—being part of that corporate identity—makes it possible for the restaurant to sell meals that cost $7 instead of $13. One could argue it's worth living with the Damons, with the Jasons, if that means Americans have affordable food.*

That's what we're known for. We're the country of plenty. But it's deceptive. We have the most food because we have the cheapest food. We have milkshakes that are 70% corn syrup, chocolate that is 60% corn syrup, ketchup that is 90% corn syrup. What we have is corn syrup. What we have are artificial flavors. We have nutritionless, nonnutritive foods: they make us feel full, give us that swelling feeling, but our bodies can't actually use any of it. Our foods are a sort of fiction. We're full on emptiness. We have exactly as much as the Siberians, the Malaysians, the Peruvians, which is *not enough*. I met a woman in Peru who had taught her children to swallow mouthfuls of air when they were hungry—to use the air to ease their hunger pains. That's all we've done, as a nation. We've been taught to swallow corn syrup, to swallow Cheetos, to swallow Coca-Cola. They're the same thing. Like mouthfuls of air. Just with some taste to them.

Louise Erdrich was talking to Lisa Halliday the other day, and Louise said, "We now see what barely fettered capitalism looks like. We are killing the small and the intimate. We all feel it and we don't know quite why everything is beginning to look the same. All across our country we are intent on developing chain after chain with no character and employees who work for barely livable wages. We are losing our individuality. Yet we're supposed to be the most individualistic of countries. I feel the sadness of it every time I go through cities like Fargo and Minneapolis and walk the wonderful old Main Streets and then go out to the edges and wander through acres of concrete boxes." When Paul French heard that, Paul said, "Michael, I'm in love with that woman, and she belongs with us. You go recruit her—I'll put in the order for her ski mask."

*Before, when I was asking about* AVALANCHE, *I was wondering what, if anything,* AVALANCHE *has actually done.*

You're wondering what I was doing at Burj Al Arab?
We do what you could call corporate sabotage, basically. My unit in Fort Wayne, we focus on advertising. Billboards, bus stop advertisements, that sort of thing. Our agenda, if we have an agenda, is for the US to revert to older forms of advertisements.

*Older forms?*

Natural forms. Fruit, for example. Why do trees grow fruit? Well, because their seeds are too heavy to be dispersed by the wind. So the trees grow fruit with the seeds inside. The fruit is advertising for the squirrels and the birds, a marketing ploy to get the squirrels and the birds to swallow the trees' product: the seeds. So, the squirrels and the birds eat the fruit, and then later shit the seeds somewhere nearby. And disperse them.
What we want, what AVALANCHE wants, is to revert to these older forms of advertisements. We want to eat at Denny's only if an actual Denny works the register inside. We want to tear down the billboards and the suburbs and the shopping malls made of fake stones. We want Myrtle Beach to be more than just a warmer Fort Wayne, which we want to be more than just a warmer Green Bay, which we want to be more than just a warmer Duluth. We want somehow to save this country from the numberless clones, from the numberless Matt Bakers and Paul Frenches and Michael Martones, to go back to a world where there is only one of me.
We also want Louise Erdrich to join us, but she has not yet said yes.

# AN INTERVIEW WITH MICHAEL MARTONE

Depending on whom you ask, Michael Martone is either contemporary literature's most notorious prankster, innovator, or mutineer. In 1985 his AAP membership was briefly revoked after Martone published his first two books—a "prose" collection titled *Alive and Dead in Indiana* and a "poetry" collection titled *Unconventions*—which, aside from *Unconventions*' line breaks, were word-for-word identical. His membership to the Order of Welsh Authors was revoked in 1999 after OWA discovered that, while Martone's registered nom de plume had been "born" in the city of Cardiff, Martone himself never even had been to Wales. His AWP membership was revoked in 2007, reinstated in 2008, and revoked again in 2010.

After his first two books, Martone went on to write *Michael Martone*, a collection of fictional contributor's notes originally published among nonfictional contributor's notes in cooperative journals; *The Blue Guide to Indiana*, a collection of travel articles reviewing fictional attractions such as the Basilica di Tito Jackson and the Site of the Great Depression of Several Emo Teenagers of 1989 (most of which were, again, originally published as nonfiction); fictional interviews with his mentor Kurt Vonnegut; fictional advertisements in the margins of magazines such as *Tin House* and *Mid-American Review*; poems under the names of nonfictional colleagues; and blurbs for nonexistent books.

But his latest book is perhaps the most revealing: *Racing in Place* is a collection of essays exploring his obsession with roller coasters, cruise ships, zoo exhibits, frankfurters, and perfume, symbols of "some widespread artificial experience." Born in Frankfort, Michigan, Martone is a self-described fashionista, and his relationship with clothing mirrors his relationship with literature: he believes the content of a story should be "perfectly tailored to its form."

In 2011 Martone was arrested outside of the Golyadkin's pub in Tuscaloosa for assaulting, allegedly, the writer Thomas Pynchon, allegedly. During

Martone's five-week sentence at Tuscaloosa County Jail, I was approved for a "noncontact visit" for our interview, meaning we could meet face-to-face, but separated by a pane of bulletproof glass, talking over yellow telephones. (It's unclear why Martone wasn't allowed a "contact visit"—typically an inmate serving time for a misdemeanor, especially one with a sentence as brief as Martone's, is granted contact visits as a matter of routine—when I asked Martone about this, he refused to answer my question.) Martone wore an orange jumpsuit, did not wear but instead held a pair of tortoiseshell eyeglasses, and had not shaved since his incarceration. I was allowed one pen and one pad of paper—nothing more.

Upon his release, Martone and his wife left for Cologne, Germany, where they will spend what remains of his sabbatical year.

■ ■ ■
■ ☐ ☐
■ ☐ ■

*In an interview with* Granta *you mentioned that for the past few years you've been at work on "fortune-telling fictions." What, exactly, are fortune-telling fictions? Can you elaborate?*

In December 1999, at the peak of all that Y2K fearmongering, my grandmother was stabbed to death by a mugger in the Lower East Side. She'd walked to the local groceria to buy canned peas and some jugs of water. As far as the police could tell—based on the spotty testimony of some frankly rather iffy witnesses—after leaving the groceria, she was offered help carrying her bags, by the mugger, who then pretended to make off into an alley with everything, only to lure her into the alley, where he stabbed her to death for the credit cards in her purse.

In the testimony of the owner of the groceria, he mentioned he had sold my grandmother a gas mask, too, which the mugger also stole, apparently, as that was never found among the cans and jugs scattered around my grandmother's body.

All of which is to say that in December 1999, at the peak of all that Y2K fearmongering, I inherited a fortune-telling shop in Alphabet City, which had been my grandmother's for over fifty years. Instead of selling it, I decided to keep it, and simply hire a new fortune teller to replace my grandmother. So I hired a tarot-reader named Neal, this moonfaced kid with gauged ears and tattooed arms, on the condition that he fortune-tell under the same name my grandmother had used: The Great Joanne. So, to this day, you can still get your fortune told in Alphabet City by The Great Joanne. All that's changed is the face.

*What does that have to do with your "fortune-telling fictions"?*

Well, I'm in New York every month or so—my daughters both live on Staten Island—and when I am, I always stop at the shop to work for a day as The Great Joanne. It gives Neal the day off—Neal, who actually has been trained as a fortune teller, and whose fortunes I would consider nonfictional, in that they're actually meant to communicate factual information about someone's actual future—and gives me the chance to write a number of impromptu fortunes, face-to-face with the both subject and reader of my fictions.

You'll know it's me, when you step into the shop, because I always play Mahler's *Titan* while I'm working. My specialty is fortunes related to fictional hauntings. If you happen to visit the shop on a day when I'm The Great Joanne, you're almost certain to have some sort of haunting foretold in your future: a stay in a haunted hotel, an accident on a haunted ferry, your unborn daughter being born someday in a haunted hospital. These fortunes, my fortunes, are always fictional, in that they're meant to communicate false information, rather than factual.

*Why hauntings?*

A few years ago my wife and I were in Mexico City, meeting with a pair of translators who were translating my wife's books. And while we were, I talked her into renting a car and driving into Michoacán, to the town where her sister Beatrice was living. She hadn't spoken to Bea in years, for various personal reasons, but she still had Bea's address from before everything went sour.

When we got to Bea's town, however, Bea wasn't there. Nobody was. The town had been abandoned: the houses, the train station, the paletas shop, they were empty, unlocked, each of them spotted with holes the size of bullets.

We later learned the cartels, or the violence of the cartels, had driven the villagers away.

*I've heard about these ghost towns: in one town, now partially underwater, a US citizen was murdered earlier this year.*

A few months before this we had been in Dublin—I was doing research for a fiction about sexbots—and we had seen the ghost estates there. The ghost estates are these vast housing developments built during Ireland's millennial economic boom. When the recession hit in 2007, Dublin found itself with a surplus of housing: hundreds of thousands of empty homes, painted, carpeted, wired for electricity. In some developments, you'll find one tenanted house for every ninety-nine untenanted—one family living in a village of empty homes.

What we saw in Mexico was a similar phenomenon, but had different causes. In Ireland, unchecked industry; in Mexico, rampant violence. Although, ultimately, I guess, those have the same cause: namely, greed.

*And it was those encounters, in Ireland and Mexico, that prompted your interest in ghosts?*

And revived my interest in identity. In Ireland, those homes were abandoned because their manufacturers were afraid of losing any more money. Well, we abandon identity for similar reasons: the way a corporation will sometimes change the name of a certain product, after that product has been connected to a baby-choking scandal, or a salmonella-poisoning scandal, or something. Or, in Mexico, those homes were abandoned because their owners were afraid of being hurt. Again, we abandoned identity for similar reasons: on the school bus, you might learn to abandon the identity you'd built for yourself as a child, learn to adopt a tougher identity, one that wears black hoodies instead of cartoony sweatshirts, wears headphones instead of earmuffs. That was my wife's experience—in middle school she transformed herself, adopted a certain identity, in order to avoid the spitwads of an older girl on the bus. She even changed her name, from Theresa to Tess—her sister followed suit, Beatrice to Bess. They insisted, *insisted*, that their parents, their friends, their teachers, everyone, all call them by these new names. Then in high school she decided she wasn't happy as Tess, so she changed her name again, Tess to Terri—her sister followed suit, Bess to Bea. Then in college she discovered she didn't have to occupy that hometown identity anymore—bullies were less of an issue—so she reverted to Theresa. "Without colors, everyone would be dressed in monotone."

*Have you ever experienced a haunting of some sort?*

My favorite story about a haunting is a story of a haunted manor right here in Alabama. There's supposedly a haunted manor on the outskirts of Headland, this estate that was razed to the ground during the Civil War—by, supposedly, runaway slaves—with the plantation's owners and the owner's children and an elderly aunt trapped inside, the ghosts of whom now haunt the site of their death. When you visit the house, supposedly you can see them, all of them: the father taking things from his dresser; the mother washing their infant with a cloth; the children reading books, staring out windows; the aunt talking to herself in an empty room. They're there every night, moonrise to moonset, haunting that second story that they died in, floating above the trees.

But here's the thing about this haunted manor, the thing that I love. *Even the house itself is a ghost*: a door only appearing when the aunt opens it, the floorboards only appearing when the children step across them, the rugs only appearing when the mother leans from a window to beat them against the house that isn't there.

*Did you ever find your wife's sister?*

We found her in a town along the coast. We had a nephew we'd never heard of. His name was Salvador. He insisted we call him not Salvador, but Doble.

*You've developed a reputation as being somewhat "nomadic." I've read that in your mid-forties you spent a year living in a motorhome, alone, driving around the country.*

From Alabama, to Pennsylvania, to Wisconsin, to California, to Colorado, to Georgia. Studying masterpieces of the forbidden art. I wasn't alone. I brought my daughters. That whole year, we lived on peanut butter and tapioca pudding.

*The forbidden art?*

The form of a hundred names. "Walkabout fiction." "Structural literature." "Narrative environments." Nobody agrees what to call it. Established literary types, however, do seem to agree it isn't "art." *The Paris Review* interviews graphic novelists now, even, but has never published an interview with Manfred Gnädinger, or Hang Viet Nga, or Niki de Saint Phalle, or Tom Every.

And maybe graphic novelists are an apt comparison. Like graphic novelists, these "story architects" use visual art in their narratives. Whereas graphic novelists use paintings or drawings or prints, however, "story architects" are sculptors. A difference of dimensions: graphic novelists work in two, "story architects" work in three. They, quite simply, build worlds.

Forevertron, for example. Or its full title: Dr. Evermor's Forevertron. That was our stop in Wisconsin. Built by Tom Every, a former demolitions expert with, obviously, some spare time, the piece includes scrap metal, antique dynamos, discarded power-plant generators, some scavenged lightning rods, theater speakers, carburetors, and part of an actual spacecraft. Forevertron is the largest scrap metal sculpture in the world, and weighing in at three hundred tons may be the heaviest fiction. My daughters were so amazed that they couldn't stop dancing. "Why are you dancing?" I said. "We want to live in this!" they shouted.

Every invented an elaborate backstory for this "walkabout fiction": built by Dr. Evermor, a Victorian-era British inventor, the machine creates a "magnetic lightning force beam" capable of launching one—specifically, Dr. Evermor, inside a glass ball, within a copper shell—into "the heavens," to flee "the phoniness of this world." His origin story includes unrequited love for an apprentice shopkeeper, an absent mother, and a troubled history with his father, a minister, their relationship encapsulated by this certain scene during an electrical storm. Dr. Evermor's launch was attended, among others, by Queen Victoria and Prince Albert.

*So this is a tourist attraction? Tourists come, buy tickets, walk around the "machine," buy themselves souvenirs?*

There are no tickets. There is no fee to see the art. There is no gate. Every is there sometimes, but otherwise you just wander around however you like.

Whether the piece was given an elaborate backstory, or has no backstory whatsoever, a compelling "walkabout fiction" always evokes some narrative for its viewers. There's Bishop Castle, in Colorado, this quirky mountainside castle with turrets and bells and a steel steeple, which, again, is free to visit. There's the Pasaquan Compound, in Georgia, and the Magic Gardens, in Pennsylvania, which, again, were each built by a lone "story architect," seemingly to fulfill some impulse or compulsion. In California, we saw the Watts Towers, Salvation Mountain, Bottle Village, The Bulb, Bowers—

*But why did you visit these? Were you considering building your own "walkabout fiction"?*

No, never. I would love to, but I'm not talented enough to build something like that.

No, instead the trip was prompted by a quote, that line that goes, "Where money is sought, art cannot be found; where art is sought, money cannot be found." Who said it, again? Bruno Schulz? Charles Schulz? One of the Schulzes. Anyway, I was tired of reading novels that had been made for profit, I was tired of reading comics that had been made for profit, I was tired of watching shows on television that I couldn't tell apart from the commercials. I wanted to experience some narrative that had been created, not for money, but for art. And in the United States, "walkabout fictions" were the only narratives left untouched by capitalism. Stories built simply to fulfill some illogical urge. A pointless desire.

*Did these "walkabout fictions" teach you anything?*

Teach me, no. But they did inspire me. For years I had been pretending that I was something that I wasn't. After touring those "walkabout fictions," though, I began practicing plagiarism again.

*Practicing plagiarism?*

Actually, this isn't the best place for me to talk about this.

*Prison?*


Listen, I do want to talk about this, but if we talk about this, it can't go into the interview.

*Okay.*

Okay. Plagiarism, as you're aware, is illegal in the United States. The United States is a capitalist nation that only tolerates capitalist practices. Ownership is a capitalist practice; plagiarism is not. Unfortunately, I'm not a capitalist. I don't believe in property, whether material or intellectual. I believe anyone has the right to tell any story: anywhere, anytime, anything. In this country, however, our right to do that has been suppressed. As a plagiarist—mmuch like a Muslim in sixteenth-century Burma, or a Jew in nineteenth-century Russia, or a Christian in twenty-first-century Somalia—practicing my beliefs in public could result in my persecution, destitution, even imprisonment. Not five weeks in the city jail. Years—*years!*—in federal prisons.

But, still, to me my beliefs are sacred. To abandon them would be heresy. So, I practice them in secrecy. Every night, I lock my office, I draw my blinds, I light my lamps, and I plagiarize Jonathan Franzen.

*Freedom?*

*The Corrections,* usually. I've already written that novel five times.

*What's the point of that?*

That's like asking, What's the point of prayer? What's the point of chanting? What's the point of lighting those candles? Ideologically, I'm a plagiarist. I believe that stories should be retold, rewritten, reinvented. To me, that practice is worth dying for.

*So you do change the book, as you're plagiarizing?*

Yes, to varying degrees. I think of books as these vast constellations of words. Whenever I'm writing—whether my own stories, or Alice Munro's, or Peter Jurmu's—my aim is always to tell the best version of that story possible, however much work that requires. If the form would be perfected by altering the structure, I alter the structure! If the language would be improved by swapping this word for that word, I swap the words! If the ideas would be balanced by overhauling the plot, I overhaul the plot entirely! If the feeling would be heightened by cutting a certain character, I cut without remorse!

I work extremely hard. And I suffer from extreme anxiety. I'm terrified some night my office will be raided, my computer confiscated, my versions of *The Corrections* destroyed by authorities.

*That seems unlikely.*

But, yet, so many plagiarists have suffered. Kaavya's novel—the copies were hunted down, carted away. Jason's *Imagine*—the books were burned, the ebooks were deleted. Pauline's *Demonic Color*—like its own characters—disappeared overnight. The story's as old as capitalism. Frank Harris was defamed for plagiarizing Marie-Henri Beyle, who was defamed for plagiarizing Giuseppe Carpani.

*I meant that that seems unlikely given that you don't publish your plagiarism. While each of those authors did. For profit.*

I'm especially protective of my *The Corrections* #4.

*Which story is it that you were researching in Ireland: the "fiction about sexbots"?*

That wasn't for plagiarism. That wasn't even for print. That was for the video game I've been writing, *A Neglected Anniversary*.

*Is the game for a console? Or computers?*

Computers. Although, I'm fluent in a number of languages, but none that a computer speaks. So working on the video game has forced me to collaborate with programmers here in Alabama. I write the script, and then the programmers make it real, bring the story to the screen. Similar, maybe, to how sometimes a writer and an artist will collaborate on a graphic novel.

*Why sexbots?*

Because they're already here, we have them, they're being made. It's not science fiction to write about sexbots anymore. It's literary. It's an examination of the moral, the social, the psychological complexities of being a twenty-first-century American human.

TrueCompanion.com was the first company to put a sexbot on the market—both the Roxxxy TrueCompanion and the Rocky TrueCompanion models, although Roxxxy costs twice as much as Rocky, which seems to indicate that Roxxxy has certain skills that Rocky doesn't.

Have you heard of TrueCompanion.com? The company was founded by Douglas Hines, an engineer from Fort Worth, Texas. Hines had a friend who died in the Twin Towers on 9/11, and afterward Hines started thinking, "Wouldn't it be great if I could create a robot with artificial intelligence and have it hold someone's personality—so, that way, I could talk to the robotic version of my friend?" So Hines obsessively set out to build a robot with that capacity, so he could install his dead friend's personality into the robot and bring his dead friend back again.

So the original concept was similar to *A.I.*: Hines thought he could sell these robots to Americans whose loved ones had died. But what happened is—this is what the company's website says—"after test marketing, the adult entertainment industry was also targeted and our robots were adapted."

Which is maybe the saddest commentary on twenty-first-century Americans I've ever heard: what their marketing research indicated, basically, was that if American consumers were offered the choice between paying $2,999 to bring back *someone they loved who had died*, or $2,999 for a sex slave, American consumers would prefer the sex slave.

*And do you think that that's the case?*

Well, of course so. We'll all use them. Sexbots will be prevalent for the same reason televisions are prevalent. Televisions are prevalent because we would rather sit in a room with a number of actual people and, instead of having a conversation with those actual people—a conversation that we know wouldn't be all that witty, necessarily, be suitably dramatic—we would rather, sitting there with those actual people, watch fake people having a scripted conversation.

That's how we live our lives: we'll always choose an ideal fantasy over a flawed reality.

Anyway, all of this is going to become a massive problem once our society begins to address the issue of robot rights.

*Robot rights?*

Currently our society is addressing the issue of sexuality rights. In the twentieth century, our society did not extend the same rights to homosexuals and bisexuals and transsexuals that were offered to heterosexuals, but our society is—it seems—coming to terms with the fact that that contradicts the fundamental principles of our society itself. Before the issue of sexuality rights, our society had to address the issue of gender rights, and before that race rights. You would think that after a while we would catch on, that we would just altogether dispose of this discriminating-against-other-humans-based-on-basically-unimportant-characteristics-of-those-humans, but humans are still animals, more or less, and will still evaluate other humans based on appearance and behavior patterns—similar to how one cow will size up another based on its size and its smell and the patterns on its hide—or at least will until our society officially recognizes that, okay, we've decided that you do need to disregard this whole race thing, or whole gender thing, or whole sexuality thing, after all.

Next our society will need to address the rights of the obese. Twenty-first-century Americans—including twenty-first-century Americans who are themselves obese—discriminate against the obese in ways appallingly reminiscent of nineteenth-century racism. How television shows use "the funny fat man," for example, the same way that minstrel shows once used "the funny black man."

After sizeism, I expect we'll next need to address clone rights. With humans being cloned even now, by the twenty-second century there will be so many clones among us that those lab-made humans are going to begin demanding the same rights extended to us sex-made.

*Do you have any interest in being cloned?*

Contemporary literature has already suffered one Michael Martone—I would never ask it to suffer several more of me.

*And, after clone rights, then robot rights?*

The prospect of humans with robots terrifies me. We're going to revive the whole slave trade without anyone even *questioning* it. TrueCompanion's sexbots, for example. These are not RealDolls. These are not inanimate objects. These are animate objects, capable of walking, of talking, of fucking, of *living*. And these are just the earliest models. By the next century, our technology may have evolved to the point where these robots do become self-aware, and then we will have animate, living, self-aware beings being bought and sold for slave labor on the public market.

It's how fifteenth-century imperial colonialism, nations sending out boatloads of settlers to invade other nations, shape-shifted into our twenty-first-century corporate colonialism: to our nation sending out McDonald's after McDonald's and Starbucks after Starbucks to invade other nations, not politically, but economically. *Culturally.* How the indentured slavery of the seventeenth century shape-shifted into our twenty-first-century version: the indentured slavery of the loan-holder, the mortgage-holder, the lifetimes-into-debt college graduate.

We keep the same systems, but give them new disguises.

*That robots will become self-aware,* ever, *seems highly unlikely.*

You must not have heard of ASIMO. Honda, the multinational automobile corporation, has been developing ASIMO since the turn of the millennium. ASIMO is an android—a robot that looks like a human—about the size of a child. Like a child wearing a plastic spacesuit: that's what an ASIMO looks like. A namesake, obviously, of Asimov.

Other corporations are developing android models too, of course. In Spain, the robot REEM, who can carry boxes. In Turkey, the robot SURALP, who can serve drinks. In Vietnam, the robot TOPIO, who is downright killer at ping-pong.

But, even among other robots, ASIMO is special. And here's why: because ASIMO models were the first robots to know that a chair was a chair.

*...The first to what?*

Even the earliest versions of ASIMO could be *taught* a chair was a chair. Engineers could bring an ASIMO into a room, point at an armchair, and tell the robot, "That's a chair," and then later when the engineers brought the robot into the room again and asked, "What's that?" the robot would say, "A chair." But if the engineers then brought that robot into a different room, and pointed at a stool, or a desk chair, or even a different style armchair, the robot wouldn't know what it was. "What's that?" the engineers would say. And the robot wouldn't know. The robot could *remember* a certain object was a "chair," but the robot couldn't *recognize* a chair as a chair.

But the ASIMO model evolved. The engineers wrote new, advanced, sophisticated coding for the robots. Here's what the robots are like today: the engineers can bring an ASIMO into a room, and point at a chair—any sort of chair, an armchair, a stool, a desk chair, a lawn chair, a deck chair, a recliner, a rocker, a glider—a chair the robot *has never seen before*—and ask the robot, "What's that?" and the robot will say, "A chair!" The robot *understands what makes a chair a chair*. And if the engineers point at something that isn't a chair—something similar to a chair, even, like an end table, or step ladder—and ask the robot, "Is that a chair?" the robot will say, "No." The robot *knows*.

And, maybe you think, "That's all an ASIMO can do?" Maybe you think, "Literally anyone could do that." But humans have it easy! Our brains just *do it*. Can you even imagine the elaborate cognitive acrobatics involved in actually recognizing a chair as a chair? In looking at an object, any object, and somehow intuiting that that object was designed for sitting?

*That sort of capacity for recognition does seem fundamental to self-awareness.*

Humans have been making automata for over four thousand years. Four thousand years ago, the Egyptians were making humanoid statues that could sing. Three thousand years ago, the Chinese were building life-sized puppets that could dance. Two thousand years ago, the Greeks were designing mechanical birds that could fly. One thousand years ago, the Iraqis were making programmable automata that could play the harp. But ASIMOs are special. This planet hasn't seen those sorts of evolutionary leaps, perhaps, since the leaps of our own species.

*To what extent is your video game,* A Neglected Anniversary, *about sexbots?*

Fregoli, the protagonist, is a sexbot. And he lives—not *it* lives, but he—in a society where robots are slaves. In the opening segment, Fregoli escapes the condominium where he's kept and begins a pilgrimage to a holy city to bargain with God, or God's human spokespeople, for his liberty.

The video game is political, in that, over the course of the narrative, players are meant to grapple with these issues of robot rights. I'm trying to get twenty-first-century Americans thinking about this now, so maybe we can avoid the whole issue altogether. But, again, humans are still animals, more or less, and I'm sure we'll make the robots suffer.

*Are you a churchgoer? Or why the plot with God?*

No, although my wife is Jain, and my grandmother, The Great Joanne, was a devout Baha'i.

As I was writing the script for *A Neglected Anniversary*, however, I was thinking a lot about the *possibility* of God's existence. I was never religious when I was younger—I've never been the sort of person who can just believe in something totally *unprovable*. In high school, and later college, I was obsessed with physics, with mathematics, with what could be *proven*. I double majored: literature plus physics. I couldn't believe in God because God was incompatible with science—couldn't translate into numbers, couldn't be explained in any scientific way.

But then I began learning about string theory—in particular the controversial M-theory—and that got me thinking about the fourth dimension.

Do you know about the fourth dimension? The first three dimensions are, of course, length, width, and height.

*A line, a square, and a cube, in other words.*

Right. Well, the fourth dimension is time. Which is difficult to imagine, visually, because time isn't spatial, unlike the others. And what makes the fourth dimension even more difficult for us to imagine is that humans, of course, are only three-dimensional.

But it's simple to imagine 2D objects. Almost all of our media comes in the form of 2D images: billboards, photographs, print on a page, pixels on a screen. Some might create the *illusion* of a 3D image—like a photograph of my wife and her sister standing in a sunny meadow with llamas, or something—but the image is still 2D.

Our brains can interpret 2D because it's only one dimension below us. 1D objects, however, are more difficult: try to imagine a line that has length but no width, something that extends in one direction while having no thickness *whatsoever*.

*...I just tried, and most definitely can't.*

0D objects are even more difficult: try to imagine a point that has neither length nor width, something that cannot be measured in any direction *but that still exists*. Are you following?

*Yes. Barely. I single majored, unfortunately.*

Don't worry, I'm almost to my point.

So, anyway, I started thinking about what it would be like for a 2D being to try to imagine 3D objects: what it would be like for a drawing of a snowman, for example, to try to visualize our own existence.

To some extent, the snowman could experience the third dimension. Let's say you cut him out and set him down there on that table. Now, if you lifted him from the table toward the ceiling—keeping him parallel to the table—a 3D representation of the snowman would form: the snowman would form a snowman-shaped "tube" in space as he moved up.

But although the snowman can move through the third dimension, it would still be almost impossible for the snowman to imagine himself in 3D. Here's why: the snowman can move through the third dimension, but for him to form that 3D object—that snowman-shaped tube in the air—he must also move through the fourth dimension, time. So for the snowman to imagine himself in 3D, he would not only have to imagine himself moving through the third dimension, and gaining height, but also imagine himself moving through the fourth dimension, time. And, for a 2D snowman, the fourth dimension is way too far beyond his cognitive abilities. He could maybe develop some *concept* of himself in 3D, but his understanding of the third dimension is limited, because the third dimension is coupled with the fourth dimension.

Which is why it's almost impossible for me, a 3D human, to imagine myself in 4D. I'm the same as the snowman: I could maybe develop some *concept* of myself in 4D, but my understanding of the fourth dimension is limited, because the fourth dimension is coupled with the fifth dimension, and the fifth dimension is totally beyond my comprehension.

*I thought this was about God.*

It is. Here's how. If the fourth dimension is time, a 4D image of me would be me from birth until death, all of the space that "I" had occupied for the time that "I" had existed. Like seeing my entire life simultaneously—a version of me as a 4D tube, like how the snowman became a 3D tube when lifted through space.

So, as a 4D tube, I might look like this: this blurry stream of infant-shaped colors that emerge on the fifth story of William Wilson Hospital in Frankfort, Michigan, on November 6, 1955, which then while growing adult-shaped squiggle across Indiana and the United States and Mexico and Ireland and Germany, and which then disappear—disappear, well, somewhere.

*So like* Donnie Darko.

So imagine the abilities of a 4D being. Again, it's the same as the drawing of the snowman. The snowman can only see in terms of length and width, so when I use an eraser to erase his carrot nose, or use my thumb to smudge his coal button, *he can't see me do it.* All the snowman sees is his carrot nose vanish, or his coal button suddenly smudge, because the eraser and my thumb both exist at a different height than he does, on a totally different plane.

Well, a 4D being would have those same abilities—could trigger a tornado in a wheat field, erase cancer cells from a girl's brain. And we would never, so to speak, even see its pencil.

And, looking at a 3D object, a 4D being would be able to see all of that object, inside and outside, simultaneously. Again, like the snowman. The snowman can only see certain parts of himself. If he looks at a 2D box, all he can see is a side of the box. But when I look at the snowman, I can see his whole outline, see even his *insides*. If I look at a 2D box, I can see *all four sides simultaneously*.

A 4D being would have those abilities, too—would be able to see all six sides of a 3D box simultaneously, and at the same time see inside the box, see the contents—could change those contents, or even erase them, without ever touching the lid.

In other words, a 4D being would be omniscient, omnipresent, and omnipotent—would see everything at once, would be everywhere at once, and could change anything at will.

It's not proof that God exists. But it's proof that it's *plausible* for God to exist, that it's scientifically conceivable. That's what I needed: an explanation for God's existence. I needed to understand how there could be something that could see inside of my head, that could see the words I was going to say before my thoughts had even fully formed.

*Does Fregoli meet God, actually—or some four-dimensional being—during the video game?*

I don't want to give too much away.

I can say, however, that Fregoli does encounter 3D beings with certain 4D properties. Ghosts, for example.

*What do ghosts have to do with it?*

Well, if ghosts are real, maybe they're just part of the 4D shape of things. Moments so prominent that they're visible from other parts of the shape. Or not even prominent moments—just moments somehow connected to your own. Like a comic-book character getting a glimpse of the panel on the opposite page when the book has been shut and the panels pressed together.

Fregoli also encounters mediums, prophets, mystics: humans with prescient abilities. Or, in other words, humans with an especially keen understanding of the 4D shape of things. 4D artists. That's what's most fascinating to me about all of this. Not whether 4D beings exist or don't exist, or what 4D beings are or aren't capable of, but *what 3D beings can do using the fourth dimension*. What if a human could see in 4D? What could they do? Well, they could see the 4D shapes of everyone, that everything ever had occupied and would occupy. And they could manipulate 3D objects in the *present*. They could read classified documents locked in a safe, spot baggies of cocaine in a human body, see a catcher in a blue jersey flipping a pitch sign to the pitcher *and* the pitcher in the blue jersey nodding *and* the third base coach in a red jersey flashing a steal sign to the base runner on first *and* the base runner on first nodding at the third base coach *and* then *know* that the pitcher was about to throw an outside fastball and that the man on first was about to steal second and that the third base coach was chewing a wad of tobacco and had a tumor developing under his tongue.

4D sight would be more than simply predicting or anticipating future events. People do that sort of thing all of the time: predicting what's inside a wrapped box, anticipating what someone will say in response to something they're planning on saying. 4D sight would be, not predicting or anticipating those things, but *knowing*.

And maybe there have been humans who have had 4D sight. Curing blindness, predicting volcanic eruptions, those would be simple for someone with the ability to see in 4D.

*How about your own prescient abilities? You've been known to make certain predictions about the future of print. In "RMS* Olympic, USS Leviathan, HMS Argus, *and Other Victims of Razzle-Dazzle" you argued, "My generation grew up with print only, so we have a certain nostalgia that may keep print around another few decades. Your generation grew up between, so I imagine your loyalties will lie between, too. But this next generation—the kids who have grown up with touchscreens and the internet and have never known anything different—they'll be the ones to bury print." The poet Piotr Zak, however—a member, in fact, of your former Order of Welsh Authors—has argued print will always be the "ruling medium."*

My wife and I honeymooned in Cologne, Germany, where we've summered ever since. We're friends with a number of expat novelists there—Paul French, Elizabeth Klemm, Jack Dowland—who can spend all night, and empty several wine bottles, arguing over the future of print. French, in particular, is determined to revive print from what he sees as its untimely death.

But what French and Klemm and Dowland believe doesn't matter. What this Zak believes doesn't matter. The ebook is an unstoppable force. Resisting the ebook is the twenty-first-century equivalent of trying to resist the printing press in the fifteenth century. French and the others sitting around arguing about print versus ebook, they're like fifteenth-century Germans arguing about scribe versus print. Yes, compared to handwritten books, print was ugly, seemed somehow inferior, had lifeless uniform characters. But whether fifteenth-century Germans thought print *should* become the "ruling medium," whether they *wanted* the printing press to replace scribes, that didn't matter. Gutenberg's printing press was an unstoppable force. And, why? Because print was quicker to publish and cheaper to distribute. And what are the characteristics of the ebook, compared to print? Ebooks are quicker to publish and cheaper to distribute. With communication technologies, quick and cheap always beats "pretty."

If we're going to revive anything, we ought to revive the scribes.

*You've been called a regionalist, an experimentalist, a disumbrationist—whom do you write for?*

In terms of heritage, I'm a cliché. A European mutt. Part French, part Danish, part Italian, part German, part British. But I don't want to write for white Americans, because that would be interpreted as writing for the Klan. And I don't want to write for men, because when you write for men that's generally seen as misogynist—Hemingway, Faulkner, Updike—which is a negative term, whereas if you write for women, you're a feminist, which is positive.

I can't write for any of the "literary" regions of the United States: I'm not from New York, I'm not from New England, I'm not a Southerner. Michigan gets lumped into the Midwest, but I can't identify with the Midwest either. It's a made-up region. And Michigan doesn't share any characteristics with most

Midwest states anyway. Michigan is all forests and lakes and snow. It's more of a Northern state, like Vermont or Montana. It's nothing like Ohio or Iowa.

What I'm saying is, I don't write for anyone, really. I write for humans. I write for h+.

*Do you consider yourself a literary writer?*

The only benefit to being "literary" is that you might get canonized and have your work taught—in other words, be skimmed by hundreds of thousands of indifferent undergrads—and thereby attain a sort of immortality, at least until you're dropped from the canon, or until the language evolves to the point where you have to be read in translation.

I'm not interested in that sort of immortality. I don't care whether my stories live a thousand years. I don't care whether they live only ten. What I'm interested in is in contributing to the evolution of literature. I want my stories to be the code of DNA that gets reused by a younger writer, gets spliced into that writer's stories, and then reused by a younger writer still. How *The Castle* becomes *The Wind-Up Bird Chronicle* becomes *The Way Through Doors*. How *Galapagos* becomes *The Children of Men* becomes *Y: The Last Man*. How *We* becomes *A Clockwork Orange* becomes *V for Vendetta*. Even if nobody is reading Yevgeny Zamyatin, people are reading Alan Moore. Through Moore, Zamyatin's DNA lives forever.

*But wouldn't a longer lifespan mean having a larger influence? And, thus, more "offspring"?*

Some novels have the heart to last a thousand years, but don't have the balls to father even a single writer. Some novels shoot blanks.

*What's your DNA, as a writer?*

My stories are the mutations. The mutant DNA.

*Like feet webbing? Six fingers to a hand?*

We need mutations to resist disease.

# AN INTERVIEW WITH MICHAEL MARTONE

Although Michael Martone never set out to revolutionize contemporary literature—and shrinks from the term "experimental"—his work has consistently defied classification, confounded his mentors, and bewildered his peers. While earning an MA at John Hopkins, Martone wrote poems the poetry students said "weren't really poems" and stories the prose students said "were more like poems than actual prose"—work that today might have been recognized as prose poetry or flash fiction. His first book, *Alive and Dead in Indiana*, was decidedly prose, but garnered over sixty rejection slips from corporate houses, indie publishers, and university presses alike: one editor remarked, "You obviously don't understand the difference between a novel and a memoir."

Born in Indiana, Martone now lives in Alabama, with his wife and their parakeet. In 2010 his twin sister, P. M. Martone, a concert pianist and spare-time cabinetmaker, had a brain aneurysm in his driveway, and has since been in a coma. When he agreed to be interviewed, he explained that he now spends nearly all of his time at the hospital, where his sister is being cared for, and that our interview would have to be conducted there.

P. M.'s room was lit by the setting sun, smelled of a recent mopping, and had been wallpapered with cards from Michael's grandchildren—P. M. herself is unmarried, and has no children. Michael offered me a chair along her bed, next to his own chair, where we sat for the course of the interview; he wore a thick gold tie that matched almost exactly the shade of her gown. His phone was plugged into the room's speakers, over which played, on repeat, at low volume, Rachmaninoff's *Isle of the Dead*. "I don't know if she can hear it," he said, "but it was her favorite piece—I'm hoping to lure her back." Throughout the interview, he held her hands.

I should also note that I began the interview with a question that, among interviewers, Michael is notorious for dodging—that question being just when and why, exactly, he began writing—and that he surprised me by actually answering. After the interview, when I asked why he hadn't simply, as usual, asked for the next question, he said simply, "P. M. was in love with a boy once, and you sort of remind me of him."

◻ ◼ ◼
◻ ◻ ◻
◼ ◼ ◻

*Just when and why, exactly, did you begin writing?*

I never wanted to be a writer. I never wanted to write stories, or poems, or fictional advertisements. What I wanted, as a teenager, was to compose the soundtracks for video games. I was obsessed with the Nintendo canon: *Mario Bros., Final Fantasy, The Legend of Zelda*. My friends, the Schieles, these cousins who lived in our cul-de-sac, they hacked my NES console, and they tinkered with the games' designs while I tinkered with the games' music. In high school we played *D&D* seven days a week—I was our group's DM—we had this idea that experience with *D&D*, experience creating these impromptu game-type fictions for a number of "players," might someday somehow translate into jobs at Nintendo.

The Schieles, they wanted to be the next Shigeru Miyamoto, or Miyamotos: they saw him as the master of their craft. Miyamoto had designed *Donkey Kong, Mario Bros., Kid Icarus, The Legend of Zelda*. We had read an article in some gaming magazine about Miyamoto's childhood, about how six-year-old Miyamoto had been roaming the woods behind his house in Sonobe when he had stumbled across a hole in the ground: the mouth of a cave. Shouting into the hole, he heard an echo. The next day he came back with a lantern, and he ended up spending most afternoons of his childhood in the cave, exploring its tunnels. Which—as this had been a formative experience for Miyamoto, had inspired the sewer tubes in *Mario Bros.* and the dungeons passages in *The Legend of Zelda*—the article said that this cave had become a sort of shrine for gamers. Gamers from the United States, from Europe, from Australia, were making pilgrimages to Sonobe to look for the cave. That was the thing: nobody knew where the cave was. Sonobe had a number of caverns that were open to tourists, but they were all way too big to be the cave Miyamoto had described.

Other artists have described similar experiences. In *Blankets*, Thompson talks about how he and his brother, when they were children, found a hole in the ground: the first day, the cave was large enough for them to hunch down and crawl inside, large enough that they even saw salamanders as they went deeper; on the second day they came back, and then the hole was only large enough for them to stick their heads inside, and they couldn't see any salamanders, the cave didn't even seem to be that deep; and, on the third day, the hole had disappeared.

Others—Onomacritus, Ts'ui Pên, Banksy in the cavern that's now called the Titan—they've described that same experience.

*Isn't Ts'ui Pên a character from* Ficciones?

Ts'ui Pên is, yes, a fictional writer from "The Garden of Forking Paths," but Ts'ui Pên is also the alias used by an actual, supposedly Canadian, writer. Pên has written one novel, *The Original Phoenix*, of which Pên infamously published only a single copy. It circulates by hand: this person reads it, and then gives it to somebody else, and then that person reads it, et cetera.

*Nobody's thought to photocopy the novel and put a couple more copies into circulation?*

I don't want to give away anything, but part of what the book is about is examining different systems of, and the differences between, cryptography and steganography. Cryptography being the *encryption* of a message, whereas steganography deals with concealing *that a message is even there*. Anyway, the nature of the novel makes it basically impossible to photocopy. "Nobody can embrace the unembraceable."

*You've seen the book?*

As an undergrad I went to this reading given at the Selhurst School by Thomas Pynchon, and afterward I asked sort of an obnoxious question, which he ignored, refused to answer, as he should have. But afterward, at the reception, he approached me with the book. "Maybe this will answer your question," he said, and then he took a biscuit from my plate, and then he walked away. Chewing my biscuit.

I didn't realize what the book was until I brought it back to my apartment, which I shared with my now wife, then fiancée. "Ts'ui Pên!" she said. "M, do you know what this is?" Back then she called me M. Now she refers to me as Von Kempelen, for reasons I shouldn't say.

*Whom did you give the novel to, once you were finished?*

Well, my wife stole it, before I had even gotten past the title page. So how it circulated was: Pynchon gave it to me, it was stolen by my fiancée, who then as my wife later gave it back to me, and I read it, and I finished it that winter, and I gave it to our mail carrier for Christmas.

*Your mail carrier?*

It was our first house, she was our first mail carrier, I thought she deserved something special.

*Nobody knows the identity of Ts'ui Pên?*

Like Banksy's, Ts'ui Pên's identity remains unknown.

*So you wanted to write the soundtracks for video games.*

Yes: so the Schieles wanted to be Miyamotos, but I wanted to be the next Nobuo Uematsu, the next Koji Kondo. I saw them as the masters of their craft: Uematsu had scored the soundtracks for the *Final Fantasy* titles, Kondo for *Mario Bros.*, *Punch-Out!!*, *The Legend of Zelda*.

By the time we graduated, the Schieles had succumbed, career-wise, to various vices: Sal to cocaine, Michael to methamphetamines, Anthony to rollerblading. They'd forgotten their Miyamoto fantasies entirely.

But I had taken three years of Japanese. And so with my popcorn-stand savings—in high school P. M. and I worked a popcorn stand at the baseball field at Plainfield Teachers' College—I bought a one-way ticket to Kyoto. I had been working on some songs, and I wanted Uematsu to tell me what he thought.

*You were just going to walk into Nintendo's building?*

Uematsu didn't work for Nintendo—Uematsu worked for Square. I respected Kondo's work, but Uematsu was who I was really after, who I wanted as my sensei.

However, I couldn't find Square's address anywhere. So my plan was, yes, just to walk into Nintendo's building, and somehow get Square's address from someone at Nintendo. After which I thought I'd pop into Kondo's office, or studio, or whatever, and at least say hello.

Incidentally, I had brought along my Social Security card—I wasn't entirely clear on what all you did or did not need, exactly, when traveling to another country—which I then proceeded to lose somewhere in Kyoto's subway system during my first night there. This resulted in my becoming probably one of the earliest victims of identity theft.

*Someone had stolen your Social Security card?*

This man, "Toru Kano," stole my Social Security number and used it to order a number of American credit cards. He then started living, quite extravagantly, as Michael Martone in downtown Tokyo. I didn't find out any of this until years later, when the financial damage this Michael, this Toru, had done, was almost irreparable.

It was that experience, though, with Michael/Toru, that inspired me to take identity theft to literature: the interviews with "William Gass," the poems by "George Burdell," et cetera.

*So that's the when and why? You began writing because of the incident with the identity thief?*

No no no, I'm still answering that question. I'd been writing for almost a decade when I discovered my identity had been stolen. At this point—in Kyoto—I still planned on being a writer, not of fictions, but of video game soundtracks.

So I should just get to the point, which is that I never met Nobuo Uematsu, I never met Koji Kondo, I never even found Nintendo's building. Like the Schieles, I succumbed, career-wise, to a vice: mine was Naoko Kasahara.

The morning after I lost my Social Security card, I was wandering around with Nintendo's address, totally lost, when I saw a sign in the window of this giant arcade. The sign said that Shigeru Miyamoto, Miyamoto himself, was giving a signing that afternoon.

The line for Miyamoto—Miyamoto wasn't even *there* yet—had already spilled from the arcade's sixth story down to its fifth, its fourth, its third, its second, its first, and then out the front doors and around the block. Japanese kids, carrying NES cartridges for Miyamoto to sign, but also a number of backpacker-looking Americans and Europeans and Australians—apparently some of those same pilgrims who came for Miyamoto's cave.

I got in line, stood there all day, never met Miyamoto—the signing ended before I'd even gotten into the building—and met a girl in line named Naoko, who I proceeded to, in a naive, cliché, very teenager way, fall wildly in love with basically instantly.

After a day, a week, a month, I'd forgotten about Uematsu altogether. I got a job in a kitchen, frying tempura, and moved in with Naoko.

*Were you still in touch with your family?*

I wrote a letter, which I later learned took nearly six months to arrive—just barely beat me back.

This was before email, of course, and before Michael Martone had the sort of funds to make an international call. The *other* Michael Martone—Michael/Toru, now living in a penthouse in Tokyo—he had the funds, but of course we weren't in touch.

And P. M. had left too. We'd bought our tickets together: mine for Kyoto, hers for Lanai. She was working on a pineapple plantation for the summer, with her best friend. And I was much closer to her than to our parents, so I really didn't feel a need to be in touch with Fort Wayne.

Anyway, I was in Kyoto, working, illegally, in a tempura kitchen. And I was living with Naoko, who kept bits of colored cloth knotted into her hair, and wore black lace dresses, and stood just under five feet tall. Naoko was a student at the international Maguire University, where her father taught economics, and her father was not entirely thrilled to learn that his daughter was dating an illegal immigrant. However, Naoko was, to some extent, rather disturbed, so at the same time her father seemed sort of relieved to have someone else taking care of her.

*Disturbed?*

The tiniest things could unravel her. We subscribed to the local newspaper, for example, and one night while I was getting dressed for work she was flipping through the newspaper when she noticed someone had clipped out an obituary, from our newspaper, as if with a pair of scissors.

I offered Naoko several reasonable theories about how this could have happened: that, for example, maybe our deliverer couldn't afford his own subscription, but some relative of his had died, so he had clipped the obituary from our newspaper, to have as a keepsake. Or maybe the publisher had printed the obituary of a missing person who had finally been assumed dead, but, shortly after the edition was printed, the missing person had been found alive, so the publisher had ordered the obituary clipped from all of the newspapers rather than pay for a reprinting.

But Naoko was obsessed. She said that the person who'd died must have been someone she'd known, that someone was trying to hide this death from her. She wanted me to run to the newspaper stand down the road, so I did, but it was dusk, and the stand was empty. Naoko only took this as a sign that her theory was correct, that someone was conspiring to hide the death.

Incidentally, at the time there was this rumor going around Shimogyo, the ward we lived in, that a multinational based there in Kyoto had been buying dead bodies from local graveyards: the story was that the multinational was operating unmarked sweatshops in Shimogyo where these dead bodies would be reanimated, brought back to life to do unpaid labor—sewing shirts, assembling electronics, et cetera—until the bodies deteriorated to the point where they couldn't function. Then the multinational would buy another batch, to replace those that had fallen apart.

Paul French lived in an apartment only a couple blocks from ours, and he claimed he had actually met one of these sweatshop undead: the man had escaped to make amends with his wife and son, French said, but as his body deteriorated, so did his brain, and his memories—when French met him, the man couldn't remember where his wife and son lived, or their names, or even his own name, only that before he had been killed in the subways, that he had hurt or abused his wife and son, somehow, and that he felt he had been brought back for a reason, to take them by their hands, to tell them he was sorry—but of course now he couldn't find them.

*Was this the poet Paul French, who told you that story?*

He was a superstar, at the time, in Japan, which is why he ended up moving to Utah, where still nobody has ever heard of him.

French was of the opinion that a work of literature had more value, more meaning, more power, the fewer the people who'd read it. Some poems, after he'd written them, he'd walk them over to our apartment, and he'd read them to Naoko—I wasn't allowed to listen, I had to wait out on the balcony—and after he'd read them, he'd burn them over our stove, so that the poems would be theirs alone. He was constantly setting off our fire alarm.

For some poems, even, French limited his audience to one. French was known for writing on this certain bridge in Kyoto—the Sanjo Ohashi Bridge, I think—for writing poems into this notebook as he was walking, and then, once he'd finished a poem, and reread it a few times, for then tearing it from his notebook and flinging it into the river below. Well, his fans caught on to that pretty quickly. They started tailing him on these walks, and when French would toss a poem over the railing, they'd go leaping in—sometimes they'd already be underneath the bridge, waiting—after the poems.

*You personally never met any of the sweatshop undead?*

Or here's another example of how Naoko was unwell. When she was younger, she'd taken a trip with her school to a museum. And one of her classmates noticed the elevator's weight limit—1,000 kilograms, Naoko said, so about 2,200 pounds—and convinced everyone to test it.

So these kids all met on the top floor of the museum—where, Naoko said, they thought they'd be least likely to encounter teachers—and then crammed into the elevator. Thirty kids almost. Some were on others' shoulders, they were packed in so tight. Naoko got shoved against the buttons—so close, Naoko said, she felt like she was trying to look through the numbers.

Then the ringleader, from the back of the elevator, called for Naoko to take them down, so Naoko nosed the button for the lobby, and it lit up, and the doors slid shut and the elevator shook and groaned and then crawled down about half a story before the lights went out.

*They had proven the elevator did have its limits.*

They were trapped in the elevator for over an hour. But of course they thought they'd never get out, so that hour felt like an infinity. Within seconds, Naoko said, half the kids were crying, and the other half were peeing.

Then came the bumping, the shouting, the flailing, the shrieking, the kneeing, the elbowing, the headbutting, the hyperventilating.

A boy next to Naoko, at some point his wrist was broken.

...

So one thing Naoko liked to do was go to this multinational's headquarters near our apartment—not the multinational rumored to keep sweatshop undead, I don't think—anyway, this enormous glass skyscraper, at the center of which was a glass elevator. Glass walls, a glass floor. The only thing you couldn't see through were the buttons—this numbered constellation—and the steel frame. Days she didn't have class, she would sometimes spend all day there, riding it up and down and up and down, watching the numbers light up and go dark, until the building closed.

She said that was her way of being brave, of showing herself she wasn't afraid of what had happened anymore, but I thought her thing with the elevator was unhealthy, honestly. I wanted to help her. I wanted to unneuroticize her neuroses, make her whole again, make her believe I wasn't going to leave her. Because I wasn't. She was my all-time favorite person, her laugh paralyzed me, her expressions slayed me, watching her humming while she washed dishes outright undid me, I wanted to spend every day with her until the two of us died, and even then I wanted the evil and probably fictitious multinational corporation to bring us back again so that we could do unpaid sweatshop labor but in that way still be together.

But Naoko was possessed by this idea that I would leave her, that I didn't love her because I *couldn't* love her, that it was impossible for anyone actually to love her, herself, as she saw herself. Which was only reinforced when she visited a Shimogyo fortune teller, who told her that things would "end poorly" between us, that I would come to "hurt her." Which was reinforced even more when she visited another Shimogyo fortune teller—hoping for some sort of counter-fortune—who told her that I was not human, not fully, that I had no "self," that "that boy that you love, something killed his identity before he was born."

And so began my war with Kyoto's fortune tellers.

*Were you ever homesick, during all of this? You hadn't planned to stay this long, originally.*

P. M. and I were in Paris a few years ago, browsing through books at Shakespeare and Company, when in a seventeenth-century almanac we found an anecdote about Scandinavian sailors: when far from Scandinavia—sailing along the coast of Thailand, or around the tip of Cape Horn—when certain sailors began showing signs of homesickness, the others would take the homesick sailors into the longboat, and row to shore, and then *bury the homesick sailors alive*, to their necks in the sand.

It was a cure for nostalgia. The idea was, if you bury the homesick sailor here— if you bury him *to his neck* in this new land—he'll forget home, become immersed.

*More holes in the ground.*

It's why we bury our dead: we want them to forget where they came from, to move on, not to haunt the rooms where we're still living.

And, in Kyoto, that was me. Culturally, linguistically, sexually, gastronomically, I had buried myself to my neck. I had forgot there were other places where I had ever even belonged.

Naoko was bothered, intensely bothered, by the fortunes these fortune tellers had given her. She spent days in the glass building, riding the elevator, coming home at night only after the building had closed. While she rode the elevator, I thought about the fortunes: I didn't believe in magic, I didn't believe in fortunes, but eventually I realized that the fortune tellers did have some power: they had not seen a truth about the future, but, rather, because Naoko was someone who believed in what they said, they had *made* a truth about the future, simply by saying it.

Like I said, I didn't believe in magic—but I knew that Naoko did. And eventually I realized that I could fight these fortune tellers with my own magic: that I could make Naoko believe things about our future the same way that the fortune tellers had.

But I was on my own. French had holed up, never came out, was working with other expats on what would become *I'll Give You This Strawberry If You Keep It a Secret.*

*That's the novel written by nine different writers?*

Right. In *The Disastrous Tale of Vera and Linus*, Ball and Björnsdóttir use a numbering system to indicate which sections Ball wrote and which sections

Björnsdóttir wrote. Or in this interview even, which is being "written" by multiple people—you and me—it will be made clear to the reader which words are yours and which words are mine. But in *I'll Give You This Strawberry If You Keep It a Secret*, nobody knows. It's never indicated, in the novel, which writer wrote which sections. I've always assumed French was recruited to write Auguste Maquet's sections: Auguste Maquet is a poet in the novel, whose narration often blends prose and poetry.

Anyway, French was basically my only friend in Kyoto, aside from Naoko, and he had holed up, so I was on my own.

What I did, for my first spell, was walk to the local fish market, where Daruma dolls were also sold. I bought a Daruma doll, and then walked to French's apartment and begged French to open the door and swore I wasn't going to stay or bother him, and then when he did crack open the door I begged him for a tube of paint, and then took the paint and the Daruma doll back to—

*Daruma doll?*

These hollow, roly-poly, wooden dolls. Zen dolls. They're so popular in Japan that snowmen there are named for them: yuki-daruma. Anyway, the dolls are sold with only the whites of their eyes: you buy the dolls blind. What you're supposed to do is, you paint one of the eyes, and then you make a wish: you ask the doll for something, like a genie. With that one eye, the doll does its magic. Then, once the doll has performed its task, you paint in the other eye, as a reward.

So I gave the doll an eye, and then told it to fight the fortunetellers, to trump the fortunes with its own magic. When Naoko got home from the elevator, I showed her the doll and told her the wish. I still remember: she *shook* with relief. She jumped on my back, kissed my neck, said we should keep the doll on the shelf above our bed until the time had come to paint the other eye.

*So the doll had worked.*

Well, for an afternoon.

While I was away that night, working in the tempura kitchen, Naoko was rooting through my backpack—she was sort of unabashedly nosy—and found the comics I had brought from the States. I had brought a few issues to read on the plane, and one was this Marvel comic, *Cancer*, about a superhero who's basically this anthropomorphic crab: the personification of the zodiac sign Cancer. At the back of each issue was always a zodiac chart—not only with the various zodiac signs, but also with each sign's *compatibilities and incompatibilities*.

And Naoko found the chart, and discovered I was a Gemini, which was supposed to be—according to this comic book—notoriously incompatible with her own sign, Pisces.

So then she was worried again.

*So back to the doll market?*

No, I knew I'd need new spells: I couldn't just buy a 500-yen Daruma doll every time Naoko encountered some unfavorable omen.

One of the other cooks was this hunched, wrinkly, ninety-something Chinese man named Xueqin, who, like me, was an illegal immigrant. Xueqin was the one who helped me counter this Western-zodiac magic. He taught me about the Chinese zodiac—taught me that by the Chinese system, Naoko had been born in the Year of the Rooster, and I had been born in the Year of the Monkey. According to Chinese-zodiac magic, Xueqin said, we were notoriously *compatible*.

It was this quest, this quest to find magic I didn't believe in to save Naoko from herself, that forced me *out* into Kyoto, out even *beyond* Kyoto—once as far as Hokkaido—to become truly fluent in Japanese, and to meet people, people other than Naoko and French and the other cooks in the tempura kitchen. Before this, I had rarely left the apartment. But now I went trekking all over Kyoto, bent over the gutters, searching for lucky coins. I wrote to P. M. in Lanai, telling her to make a sacrifice to the volcanoes, to ask them for luck for us. I went in search of monks, of astrologers, of the even merely superstitious. I recruited every backpacker-looking American and European and Australian I could find—carpenters, oyster divers, dishwashers, boxers, followers of the Cult of Cotard—and, wherever they were headed next, made them vow that they would help us. I nailed a list to our wall, made Naoko read the name of each backpacker and the magic they would do for us. Stanley Lieber, leaving for Ireland, he would kiss the Blarney Stone for us, reap some of its kissing magic. Jacob Kurtzberg, Hymie Simon, headed next for Ecuador, they would trek into the jungle for us, learn what they could of the shamans' magic. Georges Remi, headed to Las Vegas, he would mail us a box crammed with the feet of rabbits. Jean Giraud, leaving for India, she would mail us a jar of water from the Ganges, and, after India, from an island off the coast of Africa, the quill of a porcupine. Then I instructed everyone, everyone I'd met, the carpenters, the oyster divers, the dishwashers, the boxers, the followers of the Cult of Cotard, the purse thieves, the mahjong gamblers, the grave robbers, the professional mourners, the public restroom managers, the mochi vendors, the weekend moonlighters, the unemployed sunbathers, the amateur stargazers, all of them, each and every one, to scour their cities for lucky coins, to walk always with a bent head, to search under the docks and the park benches and the tables of teashops, and then to drop these lucky coins into all of the fountains and the wells and the rivers of the world, to harvest that potent magic of water, a magic, I told Naoko, that covers three-quarters of the planet, and has burrowed holes into and under nearly all of the rest of it.

...

...

*So did it work?*

What do you mean? You mean, did she come to believe that we were destined to be together?
My mistake was the tarot cards.

*What tarot cards?*

By now I was trying everything: I was teaching myself to read tea leaves, palm reading, augury, numerology, oneiromancy. While I was in Hokkaido, meeting with an astrologer, I bought an antique deck of tarot cards: Naoko had said she knew how to read tarot, and I thought that if she had her own deck, she could read our cards once a day, and that way set her mind at ease.
Naoko loved the deck—it was this nineteenth-century deck, made in Italy, with these ornate illustrations—but she refused to use it until we had learned its provenance. She said she needed to know who had owned the deck before her—whether the cards had been used by someone wicked or caring. She didn't want to use the deck if the cards were carrying "negative energy."
So I told her we would trace the origin of the cards. Which is how I ended up, finally, in Sonobe: Shigeru Miyamoto's hometown.

*The town with the caves?*

That one. I called the shop in Hokkaido where I had bought the cards, and the owner said he had bought the deck in an estate sale: this elderly mystic from Sonobe had died, and when his children had sold his belongings, the majority had been bought up by this shop in Hokkaido.

That wasn't enough for Naoko, though. She said we needed to go to Sonobe, to meet the mystic's children, to ask them what their father had been like.

*It seems like that would tell you less about whether the mystic was "wicked" or "caring" than about the children themselves: about their relationship with their father.*

Well, the mystic was dead. The children were all we had. So we took a train to Sonobe.

I should mention the owner of that antique shop had told me, "Don't go to Sonobe—this son who lives there, he is a very nasty man, very unpleasant." But Naoko insisted that we go.

What we didn't know was that the son—the mystic's son—was the co-founder and leader of CAPGRAS, a group of militant Japanese anarchists.

*Was CAPGRAS that group behind the sarin gas attacks? On Tokyo's subway system?*

No, that was Aum Shinrikyo. CAPGRAS was, unlike Aum Shinrikyo, not a cult, and, as far as I'm aware, had not killed any civilians: CAPGRAS was militant only against the Japanese government itself, against JSDF and the police.

Anyway, when we got to Sonobe, we wandered through town, peeking into empty bars and ramen shops, asking if anyone knew where we could find the Tamura siblings. We learned rather quickly that Goma, the mystic's daughter, had "gone away." When it came to Ikiryo, the mystic's son, nobody would say.

Instead, CAPGRAS found us. We were standing outside of an izakaya, across the street from a pair of housepainters, who were arguing. These housepainters were covered in gold paint—their coveralls, their boots, their cheeks, their hair—and one had a swollen eye, the other a swollen mouth. We were asking a vendor about Goma Tamura.

As we were standing there, this giant wiry man in black pants and a black jacket approached us: he was wearing a striped headband, and he had light blue eyes, which of course is unusual for a Japanese man. "Ikiryo Tamura?" he said. I stared at him. "I'm not Ikiryo," I said, "I'm looking for Ikiryo." "That's what they said," he said. "Follow me."

We followed this man to a sedan, and then—I didn't want to get in, but Naoko insisted, "Come on, get in, it will be faster!"—he drove us through Sonobe, to what we assumed would be Ikiryo's house. We passed some of those tourist caves, where backpackers stood in line, each with a fistful of yen, waiting to go inside. We passed another group of housepainters, too, again covered in gold paint, some with bruised faces—instead of arguing, these ones were simply walking along the road, back toward town. Naoko was carrying the tarot cards. She looked, for once, happy to be outside of our apartment.

"What do you want with Ikiryo?" the man with the striped headband asked, driving up front. "We have his father's tarot cards," Naoko said. "We want to know more about them." After that, the man didn't speak again.

When we got to Ikiryo's house, the man with the striped headband, along with some other men in striped headbands, tied us to a tree. "What are you doing?" Naoko shouted. After the men had left us there and gone into the house, Naoko said, "Michael, why did they tie us to this tree?" "I told you," I said, "not to get into the car."

I remember, in the yard of Ikiryo's house, there was a stone birdbath, which some children were drinking from. Then a woman, also in a striped headband, came out of the house and chased them away: like birds, these children went tearing off across the yard, weaving back and forth, making silly noises. Some birds, some actual birds, were perched on the edge of this stone well not too far from our tree—the birds must have been waiting for the children to leave, because as soon as the children had vanished, the birds flew from the well to the birdbath and took up where the children had left off.

The men in striped headbands came back outside. They were arguing. "Take them to Kawataro," someone said. "His dogs will tell us everything we need to know." "That's not good enough," another said. They came over to us. The man with light blue eyes wasn't with them. "How do we know you are who you say you are?" one shouted. "Who sent you here looking for Ikiryo?" "We have his father's tarot cards," Naoko said. "His father was a weak man," another shouted. "You shouldn't have come here. Who sent you here? Are you with the government? Are you with those capitalist puppets?" "I'm sorry," I said, "it's just that I'm in love with her, and I go wherever she tells me." Naoko kissed me on the cheek, and then the men untied us and put us back into the car.

They drove us to a farm down the road. The man with light blue eyes was back, driving again. At the farm, the men dragged us to a windmill. Kawataro, the farmer, met them there. He wore no headband and looked very afraid. The men shoved us to the dirt, tied us to the windmill, and then said something to Kawataro. He nodded, and then went off behind a barn.

Kawataro came back with three dogs—white dogs, with bloodshot eyes, more like wolves than dogs—leashed with leather straps. The dogs were fighting the leashes, barking and snarling, making the farmer stumble. The men in striped headbands stepped away—as far as the sedan, where they had parked it—as the dogs approached.

The dogs came over to us, where we were tied, and licked our faces. They sniffed my hair, and Naoko's shoes. Then Kawataro took them away again.

The men in striped headbands took us back to the car. "Let me tell you something," said the man with light blue eyes, driving again. "Those dogs are famous in this neighborhood. Those dogs hate old Hatsumi, they hate old Itoh, and they especially hate Ikiryo—and Hatsumi is the nastiest woman in Sonobe, and Itoh is a miser and a cheat, and Ikiryo beats his horses. Let me tell you, those dogs can smell anything: trickery, corruption, betrayal. Anyone untrustworthy, those dogs do everything they can to tear them to pieces. They'd kill me where I stood, if they could get at me." He pulled the car back into Ikiryo's house. "Those dogs can smell other things too: naivety, weakness, simplicity. To people like that, the dogs show their tongues instead of their teeth." The men dragged us across the yard, toward the stone well, as the man kept talking. "So if you have the dogs' approval, then you have my approval. Those dogs can smell imbalance, disharmony, something that doesn't belong, from a field away."

Then they sent us into the well.

*Into the well?*

The well was empty, no water—there was a ladder, metal rungs built into the stone.

The man with light blue eyes went ahead of us, a few of the others behind us. At the bottom of the well, we were led through a low doorway into an underground chamber. Like a bomb shelter, World War II-era, maybe, except much larger, and the room smelled like paint.

*Paint?*

The man with light blue eyes later told us what had happened. Ikiryo had hired a painting company to come and paint the underground chamber: he was planning on setting up the room as CAPGRAS's headquarters, and he wanted the walls painted black and gold, CAPGRAS colors, plus the ceiling painted with the CAPGRAS flag. Anyway, the painters started painting, but as they were, their boss let slip whose shelter they were painting—mentioned something about how the shelter belonged to Ikiryo, and about how they weren't just painting the walls, but how they'd also have to paint this flag. Well, then some of the painters became alarmed: if they'd seen CAPGRAS's headquarters, they said, that meant Ikiryo would have to kill them. The boss tried to explain that he and Ikiryo were friends, childhood friends, that Ikiryo trusted him and any of his crew, but the painters started fighting, some of them pro-CAPGRAS and most of them anti-CAPGRAS, in the room there underground. Once they were too tired to keep shoving and hitting each other, they gathered their paintbrushes, climbed out of the well, and walked back into town: the anti-CAPGRAS painters refused to ride back with their boss.

All we saw, though, when they took us down there to see Ikiryo, was the aftermath: when the painters were fighting, they had slammed each other against the walls, against the door, leaving handprints and bodyprints where the paint had been wet. The shelter looked as if, all over the room, men made of paint had been peeled from the walls.

Naoko showed Ikiryo the deck of tarot cards.

"These were my father's," Ikiryo said. Ikiryo wore a striped headband, of course, and the same black pants and black jacket. He had a fat nose, and a tattoo of a crab on his neck under his jaw. He sat on a wooden chair, cleaning a paintbrush in a metal bucket. "I sold them because I never wanted to see them again. So, why, then, would you bring them back here?"

"She wants to know what your father was like," I said. "She didn't want to use them if they had been used by someone evil."

"My father," Ikiryo said, "was a kind man," and then spit onto the floor.

"That's all we needed to know," I said, "thank you and goodbye."

The man with the light blue eyes led us toward the door. I took Naoko's hand. Naoko was smiling. But, at the door, Naoko stopped. Staring into the well, over her shoulder she said, "Your father was a mystic. If he were alive today, I would ask him: Can I trust this man I came with? Will he stay with me forever?"

Ikiryo laughed. Then he said, "Old Ikiryo wasn't the only Ikiryo with certain powers. I can tell you this much—you can stay with that boy if you want, but he is not the boy for you. Or, rather, you are not the girl for him. His life would be better, if you were gone."

...

...

*Then they just let you go?*

Of course. We were only kids, really.

But, a couple weeks later, after we were back in Kyoto, one night I came home from the tempura kitchen, and Naoko was gone. She'd disappeared, taken everything—my backpack, my money, my passport, even—everything but our one-eyed Daruma doll.

*Your passport?*

She left me nothing, so I wouldn't have the resources I would need to find her.

*Why? Because of what Ikiryo said?*

Honestly, I don't know. Probably. I think that maybe she did listen to Ikiryo—that she wasn't paying attention to everything that was happening, had misunderstood the signs.

*Misunderstood how?*

Ikiryo wasn't a mystic, wasn't a fortune teller, wasn't known for having sixth-sense abilities. But the *dogs* were. Kawataro's dogs. They were *known* for their abilities, and when they came to inspect us, they gave us their approval. That man with the light blue eyes, he had said the dogs could smell "imbalance," could smell "disharmony," but they didn't smell those on us. We were balanced, we had harmony, we *could have been happy*. For me, that's what the experience had meant: the deck was safe to use, and we were meant to be together. But for her it meant something different: the deck was safe to use, but my life would be better if she were gone.

I spent a month living with Xueqin, that cook from China, and his wife, still working in the tempura kitchen, and trying, failing, to find Naoko. On New Year's Day, I walked to a temple near Xueqin's apartment for Daruma Kuyo: every New Year's Day, any Daruma dolls bought during the year are brought to these temples, and then piled together and lit on fire. I put our doll in with the others. I didn't stay to watch it burn.

*How long was it before you gave up looking?*

Not long after that, Xueqin and his wife put me on a train to Tokyo. From the station in Tokyo, I walked to the US Embassy, and a couple days later was on a flight back to Indiana.
   But it did take—it's taken—me a very long time to process everything.

*What was that like?*

At first I tried to lose myself in music, in my keyboard, in video game soundtracks, like I'd lost myself before. But I couldn't get this new *thing* out of me that way: tones, melodies, countermelodies, I discovered I really couldn't communicate what I was feeling through them.
   P. M. was the one who gave me the notebook. She'd brought it back for me from Lanai. "I did what you asked," she said, "with the volcanoes." She'd meant me to write my songs into it, but instead I started writing about what had happened to me, about Naoko, about what it was like for me now that she was gone.
   Like French, as soon as I finished, I'd tear the pages out of my notebook, throw them into the trash. I didn't want anyone to see them. I wasn't writing for anyone else, yet. I was writing for myself.
   So that's the when and why. I began writing in the winter of 1989, in the basement of my parents' house in Fort Wayne, Indiana, because Naoko was gone, and I wanted some way to bring her back.

*So the stories in* Alive and Dead in Indiana: *in those, Naoko is—*

Yes, that's her. Just with a different name. And in Fort Wayne instead of Kyoto. That made it easier to write about, somehow, pretending it had happened in some other place.

*Have you ever been back to Kyoto?*

Once. Years later, when I was in Tokyo sorting out that business with Michael/Toru, my identity thief. While I was in Japan, I decided to take the train to Kyoto, just to see how things had changed.

I walked to our apartment, but the building was gone. So was Xueqin's building. Where the tempura kitchen had been, now there was a store that sold tools.

The glass skyscraper was still there, though. I went inside, when I saw it was—I knew Naoko wouldn't be there, but I had to look, needed to see with my own eyes that she was not in it anymore, that she was really, truly, gone. I stood in the lobby of the building, at the base of the elevator, staring up at the balconies of endless stories. It was dusk, and the elevator was lit, just a tiny box of floating light. The elevator was moving up and down, up and down, up and down. But Naoko was not on it.

# AN INTERVIEW WITH MICHAEL MARTONE

Depending on whom you ask, Michael Martone is either contemporary literature's most notorious prankster, innovator, or mutineer. In 1985 his AAP membership was briefly revoked after Martone published his first two books—a "prose" collection titled *Alive and Dead in Indiana* and a "poetry" collection titled *Dark Light*—which, aside from *Dark Light*'s line breaks, were word-for-word identical. His membership to the Manx Playwrights Association was revoked in 1999 after MPA discovered that, while Martone's registered nom de plume had been "born" in the parish of Bride, Martone himself never even had been to Man, and furthermore had written zero plays. His AWP membership was revoked in 2007, reinstated in 2008, and revoked again in 2010.

After his first two books, Martone went on to write *Michael Martone*, a collection of fictional contributor's notes originally published among nonfictional contributor's notes in cooperative journals; *The Blue Guide to Indiana*, a collection of travel articles reviewing fictional attractions such as the Trans-Indiana Mayonnaise Pipeline and the Musee de Bob Ross (most of which were, again, originally published as nonfiction); a collection of fictional interviews with his mentor William Burroughs; fictional advertisements in the margins of magazines such as *n+1* and *Geist*; poems using the names of nonfictional colleagues; and blurbs for nonexistent books.

But his latest book is perhaps the most revealing: *Racing in Place* is a collection of essays exploring his obsession with dreams, hallucinations, urban legends, and folktales, visions of "some false but true reality." Born in Fort Wayne, Indiana, Martone is a proponent of externism, and his ability to disregard flagrant logical contradictions also affects his philosophy as a writer: he believes forgery, counterfeiting, and other deceptions "reveal certain truths."

For our interview Martone invited me to a Mardi Gras ball in Mobile, Alabama, hosted by a mystic society known as the Order of Jesters. "If I have to submit to being interviewed," Martone wrote to me, "I'd prefer to do so in the company of a mystic society with a penchant for séance." When I arrived at the mansion—despite that I had met Martone before, and knew his face—finding him in the ballroom's throng of masked revelers was nearly impossible. Eventually I was approached by someone wearing a bear suit, whom I took to be Martone: the bear suit was a tribute, I assumed, to the Lost Boys from *Peter Pan*, about which Martone has written a number of essays. The bear patted my head with a paw, escorted me to the kitchen, and poured me a glass of scotch while I set up my digital recorder. I had just asked Martone my first question when someone wearing a bird mask stepped in from the patio. "Ah," the bird said, "there you are." It was Martone: this time I was fairly certain. His mask was starry—black backdrop, gold glitter—culminating in a pale curved beak. "Michael," I said, "are you with the bear?" "Matthew," Martone said, "I've never seen that bear before in my life." We asked the bear to give us a few minutes of privacy while I asked my questions. Instead, the bear poured another glass of scotch, for Martone, and then sat down at the table. The bear sat with us for the course of the interview.

I should also note that Martone, who is fond of games, consulted the bear after each of my questions, asking, "Should I answer this one or not?" Only twice did the bear shake its head no—when it did, though, Martone refused to answer those questions.

☐ ■ ☐
■ ☐ ☐
☐ ☐ ☐

*In your essay—*

Matthew, I'm disappointed you didn't wear a mask.

*I get embarrassed, wearing costumes.*

Will you wear one? Here, I always bring a spare. No? Ah, yes, okay, just hold it.

*In your essay "Myna? Starling? Budgerigar?" you said, "It's a mistake to think that we can only be influenced by existent texts. I have a theory that my* Pensées *was hugely influenced by [Jesse] Ball's* The Way Through Doors, *and that* Pensées *in turn was*

106

*hugely influential on [Donald] Barthelme's* The Dead Father.*" Will you explain what you meant by that?*

What I meant was this: I loved, truly loved, *The Way Through Doors*, but as I was reading the book I began noticing all of these parallels with *Pensées*. Not plagiarism. Just these tiny similarities, or related ideas. But a few months later I met Jesse—

*Where was this?*

Comic Con. Not San Diego, but the one in New York. I was there fulfilling an obligation for one of my alter-ego fictions. Jesse was there as just a fan. He was carrying a stack of *Fables*.

Anyway, I knew who Jesse was, but he had never heard of me. "Michael Who?" I had to repeat my name three times. Here I thought I had been this huge influence on his work—maybe even his life—and he had never even heard of *Pensées*, let alone read it. He was, however, very nice, and promised me he *would* read it, which I knew was a lie.

Then a month later he emailed me and said he actually *had* read it. And that yes, he could see some similarities between our books. And that then he had given it to his wife to read, and she had liked it, but she had said it seemed entirely derivative of *The Dead Father*. "*The Dead Father?*" I said. I had never heard of it. Neither had he. So, then both of us read it. After we did, I called him, and said, "What did you think?" "Eerie," he said. I said, "You're telling me."

*So maybe* The Dead Father *had influenced some other writer whose work you had read, and then your book influenced some other writer whose work Ball read.*

No, it's not as easy as that. This wasn't like reading *The People of Paper* and you think, hey, this reminds me of *One Hundred Years of Solitude*, or like reading *Fight Club* and you think, hey, this reminds me of *The Invisible Man*. This was like reading *Calvin and Hobbes*, and as you're reading, you're thinking, Watterson must have *grown up* on *Peanuts*. Schulz is *everywhere* in *Calvin and Hobbes*. The snowmen strips, the principal's office strips, the coming-home-from-school strips. Hobbes as Snoopy, Susie as Lucy. Calvin even looks like an early Charlie: the shirt has stripes instead of the zigzag, but other than that, Calvin's Charlie, line for line.

*That's* what it was like, reading Jesse's novel.

*I thought you said "just these tiny similarities"?*

Well, I didn't want to sound like I was accusing Ball of ripping off *Pensées*. I wouldn't accuse Watterson of ripping off *Peanuts*, either. It's just clear Watterson was influenced. Anyway, for us the situation was different, because he had never read me.

My friend Beatrice reads tarot cards. She's in the Order of Jesters, actually, although I haven't seen her here yet tonight. Anyhow, every month I visit her house, and she makes us a pot of tea—barley tea, which is my favorite—and then she reads my cards. She was the one who first suggested that maybe what I had written had been *anticipating* Ball. Like prophets: you know, Vangelia Pandeva Dimitrova, Nakayama Miki, Muad'Dib. Beatrice suggested that, in an instance of literary prescience, I already must have *known* that book that I would someday read, must have seen that book coming. *Pensées*, that was my prophecy. I wrote that predicting *The Way Through Doors*, just like Barthelme had written *The Dead Father* predicting my prediction.

Like playing basketball: when you're dribbling downcourt, you look ahead, and you see the formation the other team's taken, and you change your formation in response. Ball was going to write *The Way Through Doors*, and because I somehow was able to anticipate that, that changed how, maybe even *why*, I wrote *Pensées*.

*I'm still not sure I understand.*

Other writers have experienced this. Several years after writing *Flow My Tears, the Policeman Said*, Philip K. Dick realized certain parts of the novel were a retelling of the book of Acts.

*From the Bible? And Dick had never read Acts?*

No, never. Anyway, Dick thought this meant he must have been possessed by the spirit of Elijah. That's how he thought he wrote the novel: he *didn't*. Elijah did.

*But you think the author of Acts was somehow anticipating* Flow My Tears, the Policeman Said?

Well, I don't want to imply that Acts is fiction—stories in the Bible are supposed to be history, nonfiction, based on actual events. But maybe history *itself* can imitate fiction. Like "Theme of the Traitor and the Hero." In that story this historian is researching the events that led to the assassination of a revolutionary: the "hero." And the historian discovers that on the eve of the assassination the hero was given a sealed note, warning him he was in danger, which he never opened. And the historian thinks, that's weird—that's what happened to Julius Caesar—it's weird when history imitates history. But then the historian discovers that later a beggar said certain things to the hero that *verbatim* matched lines from *Hamlet*. And the historian thinks, okay, history imitating history is one thing, but history imitating *literature?*

*But "Theme of the Traitor and the Hero" is just a story—something Borges invented.*

Recently I spent the night in a train station, in Cobh, Ireland. Cobh is a seaport, this hilly town crammed with colorful houses, its sole tourist draw being that it was the last port of call for the *Titanic*—the last land the *Titanic*'s dock lines ever touched, before sinking somewhere in the Atlantic and drowning fifteen hundred souls. Anyway, that night in the train station, I met this elderly woman, definitely friendly and possibly unhinged, who while throwing rocks at pigeons told me a number of interesting anecdotes, including one about the novella *Futility*.

Have you read *Futility*? It's by Morgan Robertson. Its full title: *Futility, or the Wreck of the Titan*.

The plot of *Futility* is a rather straightforward rip-off of the sinking of the *Titanic*. A ship—the "*Titan*," of course—the largest ship ever built, considered unsinkable, strikes an iceberg, and, due to a shortage of lifeboats, almost everyone drowns.

What's worth noting, however, comes before the book even begins: if you flip back *past* the opening chapter, back *past* the table of contents, back *past* the title page, *there* you'll see it: "1898." The date the novella was published. Fourteen years before the *Titanic* sank.

*That's amazing.*

Or take Joe Gould. Joseph Mitchell wrote about Gould in "Professor Sea Gull," and then later in *Joe Gould's Secret*. These were nonfiction: "Professor Sea Gull" originally appeared as a profile in *The New Yorker*. Anyway, in *Joe Gould's Secret*, Mitchell relates this story that Gould had told. Gould's father had joined the army, was stationed as a medic at some camp in Nevada. And Gould's father had a friend, also a doctor, who was stationed at some camp in Florida. This was during World War I. Gould was a kid. Anyway, one morning someone from that camp in Florida called. The friend, that other doctor, had died of septicemia, or "blood poisoning," and the camp was calling to notify Gould's family. But Gould's mother wasn't home, and a servant answered, and the servant misunderstood. She thought that who had died was *Gould's father*. When Gould peeked into the kitchen, she was crying, and said his father had just died from septicemia.

Gould went into shock. He went to his room, and shut his blinds, and sat on his bed in the dark without moving for the next seven hours, mourning his father.

Anyway, when his mother got home, she called the camp in Nevada and straightened everything out. But here's where things get like "Theme of the Traitor and the Hero": a month later his father was honorably discharged, and returned to Delaware, and went back to practicing medicine. But, just a few days after he had returned, he got sick and died—from septicemia.

Again, history imitating fiction: the servant created this fiction that his father had died from septicemia, but in the end she wasn't wrong, only premature.

*Wasn't Gould a pathological liar? I've read Mitchell's book. Gould claimed to have written the longest text in the English language,* An Oral History, *a supposedly nine-million-word collection of transcriptions of conversations. Mitchell later discovered* An Oral History *actually consisted of only a few chapters, which Gould had rewritten hundreds of times—appearing to fill hundreds of notebooks with material for* An Oral History, *while simply rewriting the same few pieces.*

There isn't any proof that the *Oral History* didn't exist. Mitchell suspected that, but never directly confirmed that with Gould. And Gould may have had reasons for wanting him to believe it didn't. He had been putting pressure on Gould to publish the *Oral History*: he would set these ambushes in his office, where Gould would stop by to visit, and then one of his editor friends would "happen" to show up. Gould was horrifically shy—pretending his book was fake may have been the only way to preserve his privacy.

But let's say Mitchell was right, and Gould never wrote the *Oral History*.

Well, what's the title? An "oral" history. Mitchell said Gould's true genius lay in oral storytelling anyway. So in that sense Gould did "write" the *Oral History*: he told it to Mitchell, over a period of decades, in their countless conversations. If we don't have it, that's because Mitchell never wrote it down.

*So those are your "reverse influences." How about "forward influences"? I've read that in your mid-thirties you spent a year living in a cabin, alone, with only three books.*

In Minnesota. *Frankenstein, Phantastes, Somnium.* That's what I read that year. Over, and over, and over again. I drank frozen stream water, I ate smoked venison and canned peas, I wore the same sweater every day, I grew a beard, and I read those novels.

Yes, as stories, they aren't particularly gripping—actually, they're remarkably boring—but, as stories, they achieved the ultimate. Those novels created new *genres*. Horror, fantasy, sci-fi: that's arguably where they began.

That's what I went there to study. To try to learn how to do. How to invent an entirely new category. I cannot imagine a more astonishing feat for a story to make. There is nothing greater. Reading *Action Comics* #1, I get nauseous with jealousy.

*You own* Action Comics *#1?*

In 1939, my uncle bought a copy for a "grimy penny" off a kid moving to a new city. In 1989, he gave me a photocopy. Every morning since, I've read *Action Comics* #1 with my eggs and toast.

*Was Borges a "forward influence"?*

"A mere handful of arguments have haunted me all these years; I am decidedly monotonous." Borges was the master of the premise. He came up with dazzling story concepts, but was incapable of actually following through—incapable, or too lazy. So instead he just wrote stories about the stories. His fictions are like dares. He'll present a certain premise as if to say, *somebody* ought to write this sort of thing, but it's not going to be me.

But the premises are brilliant. Take "Tlön, Uqbar, Orbis Tertius," in which he proposes writing a series of fictional encyclopedias about the history, culture, and languages of a fictional planet. These encyclopedias, he suggests, could be invented by one generation, expanded by the next, refined by another, et cetera. Much like stories once *were* written—by a community of storytellers, over multiple generations—before copyright laws turned stories into property. Even if you think of a way to improve *The Corrections*—a more powerful line for Denise to say on page 231, a different anecdote to include about Chip's background in academia—you can't. Franzen "owns" it. It's never going to change. It's dead the moment it's printed.

Storytelling was communal once, but we've lost that now. That's what Borges is mourning in "Tlön, Uqbar, Orbis Tertius." We're trapped in a nation of stillborn literature.

*You mentioned your "alter-ego fictions." What inspired those, originally? Do you remember?*

Justin Janus, probably. A friend from high school. The summer after graduation, Justin moved to Alaska. He wanted to work on a crab boat: he had heard deckhands could earn a triple-digit salary in a single summer, hauling in crabs sunrise until sunset, sleeping on the boat.

When he came back that next fall, though, here's what he said had happened. He drove a week straight, not stopping for anything, pissing in a jar as he sputtered along the highway, and then his pickup died just outside of Anchorage and he had to hike into town. And once he got there he couldn't get a job—not on a crab boat, not on a shrimp boat, not on a clam boat, even—and was sleeping in a hotel and blew all of his money the first weekend he was there.

The problem was, like Gould, Justin was horrifically shy. He had trouble introducing himself to the captains of these different boats: he would get nervous, mumble, give off this aura of incompetence. But, that next week, something strange happened. One night a pair of girls standing outside the hotel asked who he was. And—broke, defeated, unemployed, alone at the end of the continent—he acted on some bizarre impulse: he introduced himself as "Jasper Jinx."

But when he did? No mumbling. Pretending to be some other person, he wasn't nervous what the girls would think of him. It wasn't Justin Janus who would be judged, only Jasper Jinx.

So he kept doing it. He started telling anybody he met that that's who he was. And a few days later he got a job on a clam boat and sailed off into the Pacific, where his captain turned out to be an alcoholic and an insomniac and borderline Ahab about these clams. And there was almost a mutiny, but then there wasn't, so Justin came back to shore with just enough pay to buy another pickup and the gasoline to get him home again.

When he got home, though, he wanted us, too, to call him Jasper Jinx. We'd known this kid since seventh grade—we'd been trick-or-treating with him, played basketball together, built a rope swing in his yard—but now he wanted us to forget that kid altogether. He said he liked who he was when he was Jasper more than who he was when he was Justin. Well, we said, you're crazy. We're not going to call you that. You'd sound like a supervillain. But he insisted. He even had his name changed, legally. His parents convinced him only to change the given name, not the surname, but, still, now his license said Jasper Janus. Our friends kept calling him Justin, mocked him nonstop about the "Jasper" on his license. But I thought, huh. Maybe there's something to that. Maybe he really is different from that kid we knew before.

*Were you already writing?*

I had been writing since middle school. And I had been taught—in school, by my mother—that fiction was something on the page. But what Jasper had done showed me that the boundaries weren't where I had thought, that fiction also could be something in our lives.

So I decided to make my own alter ego. But that turned out to be almost impossible. I could change my name, or wear a weird hat, but I couldn't convince *myself* of the fiction. Like that line from *My Life*: "I had always hoped that, through an act of will and the effort of practice, I might be someone else, might alter my personality and even my appearance, that I might in fact create myself, but instead I found myself trapped in the very character which made such a thought possible and such a wish mine."

So I decided to practice through letters. That summer that Jasper was gone, one week all of my friends had driven to Minnesota to camp on Lake Superior. And this girl from Idaho was there visiting her father, and we had a weeklong romance and then had swapped addresses and she had flown back to her mother. We hadn't written yet, so I decided to send her some letters, and through those letters to create a fictional life. I had to use my own name: she already knew me as "Michael Martone." But the Michael Martone I told her about in the letters didn't actually exist. The fictional Michael Martone had an allergy to citrus, had an affinity for parakeets, had played the clarinet, had a twin who had died in his mother's womb.

*I've read that you—*

No. Wait. Maybe Jasper wasn't the inspiration. I just remembered an incident from middle school. Yes, *that* was probably my first alter-ego experience, albeit inadvertently.

In middle school I desperately wanted to fit in, but I really didn't stand a chance. I had glasses twice the size of my face, wore extra-large shirts on an extra-small body, and took precalculus classes once a week at a college campus nearby. I played in the band class, trumpet, which made things even worse: at our school the trendy thing was choir. At the tryouts for basketball, during free-throw drills, I made zero out of ten.

Probably the most popular student was this kid named Dustin Eidola. Jasper was Justin, back then, obviously. They were best friends. Kids loved referring to them as a duo. You know, "Dustin and Justin." Everybody liked Dustin, because he owned piles of video games, and never missed free throws, and actually could fill out an extra-large. He was colossal, for our age. At lunch I always sat with the popular kids—none of them had any idea who I was, but they let me hang around anyway—and he would make these jokes about sexual organs I hadn't even known existed. Everything I know about sex, I learned from him. That's all it took: a year of his jokes.

Anyway, he was incredibly depressed actually, and on lots of meds, and then one week after spring break he stayed up three days without sleeping. He came to school, still, but—this is what his parents said later on—at night he'd just play video games. I'm not saying they killed him: his parents said he played them all night *because* he couldn't sleep, not vice versa. Anyway, sometime during the third night his heart stopped. His parents found his body in the morning.

*That must have been traumatizing, even if you weren't actually friends.*

The really traumatizing thing came later. That summer, I finally fit in with everyone. I had been idolizing these kids since kindergarten: suddenly my house was their hangout. They would bring over these records I had never even heard of—*Vision Thing, Three Imaginary Boys, Speaking in Tongues, Forever Michael*—and we'd eat popcorn my mother had made and play Atari.

Which was good for me. I became happier, less timid. I was the mascot of our group, their clown. I even briefly dated an eighth grader. We never kissed, but we did hold hands, and at the time that was an enormous victory.

Sometime during seventh grade, though, I realized what had actually happened. When Dustin died, he had created a vacuum. And I had filled it. I had essentially *become* Dustin: I was the new "friend with video games," was the new "friend with lots of jokes." Because my sense of fashion was nonexistent, I even wore the same size shirts. I had become a fiction. They weren't friends with Michael Martone: they were sustaining their friendship with Dustin Eidola *through* Michael Martone, using me as their medium. I'm sure they felt guilty about his death—I even felt guilty, and, as you pointed out, we hadn't even been friends—and the way they coped was by being especially friendly to this new Dustin. When that eighth grader held my hand, she was holding it because it was Dustin's. For her that was the allure.

When I realized that, I broke up with her. I didn't date anyone again until I had graduated and gone off to college. I didn't want to be anyone's Dustin.

*You later learned to embrace that sort of transformation. In college you and your friends enrolled a fake student, John Smith, and even attended his classes. And when Neal Bowers wrote a book about his hunt for someone who had plagiarized his poems, you then began publishing poems under the name Neal Bowers—essentially donating to his oeuvre.*

Indonesia has a set of unwritten laws, adat, under which ownership of art isn't recognized. Here we take for granted that stories are things that have owners. In Indonesia, there is no "intellectual property." Whether you wrote *Rabbit, Run* doesn't matter. I can sell a million copies of it without paying you any royalties whatsoever. I can rewrite its ending, or retitle it *Brewer, Pennsylvania*. And why shouldn't I be able to? Author, copyright, the concept of an "oeuvre"—these are not inalienable rights. They're a cultural aberration.

Anyway, that isn't true, exactly, about Bowers. That is what I told everyone at the time. And I had actually been planning on doing that, but then one afternoon my uncle called—I'd just started teaching at Harvard—to say my cousin Maddie had written these *astonishing* poems. I *had* to read these, he said. So I said, well, okay, send me some. I wasn't thrilled. I knew he wanted me to validate them, to tell him they showed this promise that, of course, they wouldn't.

But when the poems came, I was blown away. Not by all of them: most were your average seven-year-old's poetry. A mesostic about ghosts, an acrostic about snowmen, a haiku about her Dalmatian. But some of the poems were among the most brilliant I had ever read. Especially by a second grader.

Of course, nobody was going to publish a poem by a seven-year-old. Wearing her nametag, the poems were unpublishable. But I was interested in the merits of the poetry itself. So I sent the poems off to some magazines with Neal's name attached instead. I thought, if Neal had written them, would anybody publish them? It turned out people would.

*What did your uncle say when he found out?*

I never told him. He would have been upset that I had published the poems under Neal's name. I just said, "Look, the poems were okay, but not bad for a seven-year-old. Tell her to keep at it."

*Have you told anyone this before? Publicly?*

I don't consider this "publicly." My uncle doesn't read literary magazines, especially author interviews. *Writers* don't even read author interviews. And anybody who does is only skimming. I can say anything I want to here, and it wouldn't matter. Anyway, let's blame the scotch.

*You've "written" a number of alter egos since: Andrew Carlssin, Jara Cimrman, Rudolph Fentz, John Titor, Von Helton, Leonard Lewin, Boxxy.*

I've abandoned more than I've finished. I sometimes worry my unfinished selves will come back for me, for a sort of haunting, like in Pirandello's *Six Characters in Search of an Author*.

*Before you've said you think of you and your alter egos as a mobile: you as the crossbeam, your alter egos as the objects hanging by strings.*

"It is my image that I want to multiply, but not out of narcissism or megalomania, as could all too easily be believed: on the contrary, I want to conceal, in the midst of so many illusory ghosts of myself, the true me, who makes them move." Ideally, whoever's in the crib below doesn't notice the crossbeam, only the spinning characters. I'd rather not exist at all, but the characters do need something to hang from.

*So are alter-ego fictions the new genre? The "entirely new category" you hoped to invent?*

Not hardly. It's an old genre. *SunDreamMoonColors*, for example, was written in the seventeenth century. Have you heard of *SunDreamMoonColors*? It was published by an Irish writer named Wilmore. Several years later, however, Wilmore announced he was merely a nom de plume: he had agreed to be used so by another writer, Busoni. So began the trail of nom de plumes, all actual people, each of whom stepped forward as the "author," Busoni, then Zaccone, then Sailor, then Picaud, et cetera, each outing the previous "author" as merely a nom de plume. This went on for dozens of "authors," into the eighteenth century.

My favorite contemporary working in the genre, though, is Sophie Calle. She once asked Paul Auster to invent a fictional character who "resembled" her. So he did: he used her as the model for Maria Turner, a character in *The Book of Illusions*. Like Calle, Turner is an artist. But the art Turner makes is fictional—isn't based on anything ever actually made by Calle.

After the novel was published, however, Calle then *actually created* the art attributed to that fictional self in the book.

*Speaking of your alter egos, I've heard you were recently exiled from Facebook.*

Banished personally by the dictator himself. Zuckerberg's underlings discovered that I was operating, simultaneously, nineteen fictional entities on the site. Zuckerberg deleted my fictions and banished me for life.

*Do you ever work with Twitter?*

By tweeting fictional quotations, generally. @NRA: "Rage is a powerful energy that with practice can be transformed into fierce compassion," supposedly by Thomas Jefferson. After the death of Osama bin Laden: "I mourn the loss of thousands of precious lives, but I will not rejoice in the death of one, not even an enemy," supposedly by Mahatma Gandhi. On the occasion of the collapse of our economy, and the world's, into the Great Recession: "Owners of capital will stimulate the working class to buy more and more expensive goods, pushing them to take more and more expensive credits, until their debt becomes unbearable: the unpaid debt will lead to bankruptcy of banks, which will have to be saved by the government and nationalized: the state will take the road that eventually leads to communism." Supposedly, of course, by Mao Zedong.

*Why attribute the quotes to actual people?*

Who would read *Dianetics* if it hadn't been published as "nonfiction"?

*You've written several essays, notably "About-Face," on the mythology of the superhero. I've heard Pynchon was the one who got you into comics, when you were rooming together in New Mexico.*

No, I was reading comics long before Ruggles. When I was a kid, my uncle owned a shop that sold comics, baseball cards, and Cornish memorabilia. And every few weeks I would go over and help him run his shop. He paid me with comics. He didn't have to—for a kid, helping out at a comic-book shop isn't work, it's the ultimate vacation—but he did anyway. So I earned almost every issue of *Métal Hurlant,* most of *Asterix,* most of *Tintin,* a lot of Tezuka.

Speaking of Pynchon, he's worked in the alter ego genre too, but *nonfictionally.* Pynchon claims that in his mid-twenties he was abducted by aliens, who replaced him with a changeling, a fake human who assumed the name "Thomas Pynchon" and published his first novel, *V.* Meanwhile, Pynchon's experience onboard the alien spacecraft was what inspired his next novel, *The Crying of Lot 49,* which he published once he had returned and reassumed his identity.

*"Changeling"?*

Changelings. Before aliens, fairies were the ones who would use them. Fairies would abduct a newborn, and then replace the baby with an imposter. The only way to prevent this was to name the baby: the fairies could only steal a baby that was nameless.

The name of this syndrome is Capgras: it's a psychological disorder where you're actually prone to these delusions. You become convinced that somebody has been replaced by an identical imposter, or imposters.

A related syndrome is Fregoli: it's a psychological disorder where you become convinced that multiple people, different people, are actually the same person, somebody in disguise.

*In that essay you label Neil Gaiman's* The Sandman *"a formal initiation of the superhero pantheon into the realm of world mythology." In what sense are superheroes a pantheon?*

In the sense that they were written in the same way as historical mythologies: by a community of storytellers, over multiple generations. And that these gods—sometimes immortal, always superhuman—intermingle, share a fictional universe, play a role in each other's stories.

So, yes, what I said before wasn't true. We're not "trapped in a nation of stillborn literature." Our *novels* are stillborn, but not our *comics*. At DC and Marvel, writers can retcon the myths, issue to issue: rewriting the backstories, reinventing the characters. This does occasionally result in a *Crisis on Infinite Earths*, but that's not unbearable.

*Action Comics* #1 was 1938, *Detective Comics* #27 was 1939, *Whiz Comics* #2 was 1940, *Captain America Comics* #1 was 1941. Superman, Batman, Captain Marvel, Captain America came to life, and "Tlön, Uqbar, Orbis Tertius" meanwhile was published in 1940. Coincidental? Possibly. But superhero universes *are* "Tlön, Uqbar, Orbis Tertius."

Is that where you were headed? Beat you to it.

*You also mention, but never identify, "three types" of alter egos.*

DC and Marvel often publish "origin stories": how Hal Jordan became the Green Lantern, how Jennifer Walters became She-Hulk. Sometimes the alter ego is forced onto the character by a backfired experiment, a freak accident, chance: Spider-Man, the Hulk, the Fantastic Four. Similar to Michael becoming Dustin, maybe. Others create it, choose to become it, to undertake some task: Batman, Iron Man, Green Arrow. Like Justin becoming Jasper.

*Then some are born with their abilities?*

Superman, Wonder Woman, Hellboy. Yes, that's the third type. Chance, choice, and nature. In other words, Muhammed types, Buddha types, and Christ types. In their respective traditions, Muhammed was a normal person until being visited in that cave by an "angel," Buddha chose to abandon the palace for "enlightenment," and Christ was born the "Son of God."

You could argue the second type is just a subset of the first type: that Bruce becomes Batman because of seeing the murder of his parents, or that Siddhartha became Buddha because of seeing "the four signs." But they had a *choice*. Bruce could have dealt with the deaths like a normal person and then spent his life in luxury at the mansion, but instead he transformed himself into something mythical and spent his life getting revenge on the underworld of Gotham. And even after seeing "the four signs," Siddhartha could have dealt with the existence of "aging" and "sickness" and "death" like a normal person and then spent his life in luxury at the palace, but instead he transformed himself into something mythical and spent his life battling demons, associating with murderers, untouchables, cannibals: the underworld of India. In contrast, Spider-Man and Muhammed were transformed by events. Both were orphans, raised by an uncle and aunt, normal people—until that spider grants Peter powers, whether or not he's interested in having perfect vision and a sixth "spider" sense—until that angel grants Muhammed powers, whether or not he's interested in becoming literate and hearing voices from another world.

*You do see these three types in literature, too: Dr. Jekyll becomes Mr. Hyde after an experiment backfires; Edmond Dantès chooses to become the Count of Monte Cristo, and avenges himself through his alter ego; and Frankenstein's monster is born as a superhuman, but tries to live among the humans, to blend in, to become a "Clark Kent."*

Here's what wasn't coincidental about the timing. Superheroes appeared in a climate of strong nationalistic fervor, in the months leading to World War II. We were a nation composed almost entirely of first- or second- or seventh-generation immigrants: we had no historical mythology to supply us with premade gods. Superman, *Action Comics* #1, created this craze for superheroes. By the time the US had entered the war, a number of our most celebrated gods had already appeared: Starman, Hawkman, the Spectre, the Flash. And they all "fought" with us.

But those superheroes each lived in a separate imaginary universe. There wasn't any pantheon yet. Only in the '60s, when superheroes began referencing each other—and eventually making appearances in each other's comics—did a true pantheon form.

*But how did* The Sandman *initiate superheroes into "the realm of world mythology"?*

Have you read *The Sandman*? *The Sandman* was written for DC, which meant Gaiman got to use characters from the DC Universe. But *The Sandman* isn't about superheroes. *The Sandman* is about gods. In *The Sandman*, gods exert power relative to the worship they receive—are born with their first believer and die with their last. And Morpheus, "The Sandman," is constantly encountering the struggling gods of dying myths. Ra, Sigyn, Ishtar, Baba Yaga, Susano-O-No-Mikoto. The Furies, who become a plurality, something many-named: the Fates, the Hecateae, the Eumenides. Meanwhile, Morpheus also encounters gods from the superhero pantheon: Doctor Occult, Phantom Stranger, Element Girl, Mister Miracle, Wildcat. Normally when gods from a historical mythology show up in a comic, the gods are just guests in the superhero universe, a sideshow to the main event. But in *The Sandman*, superheroes are the sideshow, too: just another pantheon of gods wandering around the story. Etrigan the Demon bargains with Beelzebub and Lucifer; Fury meets the Furies; Superman, Batman, and Martian Manhunter attend the same funeral ceremony as Odin, Bast, and Titania. Our new gods shake hands with the old gods, publicly recognizing superheroes as our official pantheon.

*But why did we choose these gods?*

Because that's our story. We're not a nation where people live in the same town from age zero to seventy. Identity isn't static here. Even our stories that aren't about superheroes are about superheroes. In "Plainface," Plainface has an ability to assume the identity of a stranger's acquaintances, actually to *become* those other people. In "Sarah Cole: A Type of Love Story," the first-person narrator wears third-person masks. When you look for it, it's everywhere: *Moby Dick*, *East of Eden*, *The Great Gatsby*. We're a nation where you can't be who you are forever.

Then there are my alter egos. Theodor Geisel, Allen Konigsberg. Even Michael Martone. I've never felt much like "Michael Martone." I feel sometimes like I've been wearing a costume my whole life. I had to put on "Michael Martone" to do things I couldn't do myself. But now I can't take it off. I forgot where the zipper is. I'm stuck in it.

*But you're you.*

But who is this "Michael Martone"? Who is "Matthew Baker"? Is he different from "Matt Baker"? Is he different from this "Crow" I've heard you answer to? From this "B"?

In Ireland, I also went to Dublin, to give an unsolicited reading at Trinity College. While there, I visited a certain art gallery, where Francis Bacon's studio is indefinitely on display—

*Francis Bacon? The philosopher? Who died of pneumonia, after stuffing a bird with snow as part of some experiment?*

No, not the scientist, there's another Francis Bacon, an artist, who painted triptychs and was obsessed with *Battleship Potemkin* and died in relatively warmer conditions. Bacon's studio was notoriously chaotic: stacks of photographs spilling across the floor, crusted cans spiked with paintbrushes, sketches trampled with bootprints, buckets teetering on other buckets, toppled easels, empty cardboard boxes lying upended among dropped cloths and squeezed tubes and dirty bowls and half-buried trowels and plastic caps smeared with paint and a weathered door, with a battered window, hinges fixed to nothing, leading to nowhere. The clutter was deliberate: that's how Bacon preferred to work. In the embrace of inanimate objects. Cramped, and tripping.

After Bacon's death, the studio was donated to this gallery, who—instead of selecting certain artifacts to display and then packing the rest away into storage—decided to relocate the studio, *in its entirety*, to the gallery. The idea was incredibly ambitious and arguably psychotic. Here's what they had to do: over a period of months, every object in the studio was inventoried. Imagine! *Every object*, listed, named. But, of course, that wasn't enough. To remake the studio, they needed to know, not just what objects were there, but *the position of every object in relation to the other objects*. The angle. The distance. The shape of the ridges in the crumpled fabric of this glove. The whole landscape, mapped by these cartographers of an abandoned world.

Then, piece by piece, the studio was moved to the gallery, where the studio was rebuilt, in *that exact same constellation of objects*, for display. Perfectly organized. The same chaos.

And if that can be done, couldn't we relocate a person the same way? Couldn't memories be relocated to a new body, transporting that identity, that person, that soul?

*Aren't we more than memories?*

That thing you refer to as "yourself" is just a collection of memories: an incomplete set of sensory impressions recorded by an "organic data-collecting machine." My own "self"—my shy nature, my belief in samsara, my preference for barley tea—all result from my own "recordings."

The way Salinger's personality changed, drastically, after being in an accident, recording a new set of sensory impressions: the sound of his daughter breaking her jaw on the steering wheel; the touch of a stop sign slicing the skin of his arm; the sight of a world upside-down.

*Or Mark Hamill, "Luke Skywalker," after his own crash.*

The way someone's beliefs might change after recording someone talking: about, for example, the inconsistencies of certain sacred texts. The way someone's preferences might change after an illness: the way mine did, having thrown up a snack of walnuts, and recording the taste of that on my tongue, the smell of that on the floor of my classroom, the sight of other kids recording similar sensations because of what my body had done. I don't eat walnuts anymore. I *can't.*

My personal data-collecting machine is constantly recording. Smell, I tend to notice only when eating. Taste, too. So the senses primarily responsible for my relationship with the world, then, are sight, and sound, and touch.

So how then would my "self" change if I were colorblind? How if I were deaf? How if my skin were especially sensitive to light, to perfume, to wasp stings?

*In "Shandmaske, Shandmaske!" you said you're "haunted" by the "limited perspective of the self."*

Honestly, my biggest regret in life is that I have only one—that I'm only able to experience our universe from the perspective of a single machine. My personal data-collecting machine is drawn to visual arts. Is that because it experiences color differently than other data-collecting machines? Do its eyes simply record a world more saturated with color?

The color my personal data-collecting machine loves most is orange—specifically, the saffron color of robes worn by some monks in Asia. But when other organic data-collecting machines experience this color, what color do they see? Why didn't I see the color green—specifically, the green of ripe limes—in the way my mother did, who adored it so much as to paint the walls of both our kitchen and her bathroom with thick coats of it?

*Still, saying the "self" is determined entirely by memories does seem somewhat reductive.*

What if we could replace the memories kept in your brain with the memories kept in mine—erase all your data, and then transfer all my data to you? Wouldn't you then *become* Michael Martone? My new "self"? You wouldn't eat walnuts—I can promise you that much.

Our memories have an awful power over us. That's what we have language for: to communicate sensory data to other machines. We *need* that. My father didn't like to talk, so he drank and drank and drank to dull the memories that he kept. My mother, though, taught me if you talk about a memory—communicate it even to just *one* other person—that can dull it too.

But our memories are flawed, of course. Our machines are incapable of storing infinite amounts of data: every night while we sleep we dump most of our sensory impressions from the day into that "oubliette" of our dreams. And even the memories that are preserved become defective, expire eventually. The way a broken bottle, not originally recorded by any of your senses, might suddenly materialize in the memory of a wedding at the beach, become a central part of that memory, this thing that was never there. The way you might have a memory from your childhood of the smell of a bowl of cereal caught by the breeze—the only surviving memory from that year, that milk-cereal-marshmallow smell, which, in the memory, smells extraordinary, perfect, impossible, far better than the cereal ever could have actually smelled.

When I was a kid, my mother wanted to be a writer. After decades trapped in her personal data-collecting machine, she decided to communicate the data she had collected to others trapped in organic data-collecting machines of their own. Nothing, she thought, could be more important than that. So for years she told her stories. She wrote them on paper. She spoke them out loud. She convinced others to reenact them, to perform them for audiences of others still. She existed only to record, and then to communicate those recordings.

But in the end she discovered that she had no story to tell. Other organic data-collecting machines were bored by her stories, uninterested in her experiences, ignored the memories she attempted to communicate. And that, she said, was her failure. She had recorded nothing of value. She had seen nothing of use to anyone, had touched nothing of significance. For all the preserves in the jar of her skull, none were worth the tasting.

*This thinking seems very Dickian.*

I do admire Dick's novels. He's a brilliant storyteller. That's why his books translate so well into film. That's actually how I got interested in him: I started noticing that every time I saw a sci-fi movie that I liked, at some point the credits would say, "Based on a story by Philip K. Dick." *Blade Runner, Total Recall, Minority Report, A Scanner Darkly. The Matrix*, unofficially. *E.T.* wasn't him—*Terminator* wasn't—but aside from those he was behind *everything*. Of course, he's not a very good writer. That's why he wrote in the sci-fi genre: with sci-fi, you can get away with being a bad writer as long as you're a good storyteller. The literary genre is the opposite: with literary work, you can get away with being a bad storyteller as long as you're a good writer.

*Literary fiction isn't really "genre" though.*

Literary writers think "genre" writers are a bunch of hacks using genes they stole from Asimov and Stoker and Tolkien to clone their own stories. They think that every adventure novel is the same, every mystery novel, every romance novel. Which isn't wrong—most romance novels are basically identical, are totally derivative of every romance novel that's come before—but what literary writers need to acknowledge is that literary novels *do the same thing*. "If ever asked, what's more useful, the sun or the moon, respond, the moon—for the sun only shines during daytime, when it's light anyway, whereas the moon shines at night."

Next year, every literary novel published, here's the story: it's almost guaranteed to be realist; it's almost guaranteed to be about a family; it's going to have more symbols and metaphors than fantasy books have dragons; and, aside from maybe a few slight psychological shifts, basically nothing is going to happen.

I blame Hemingway. Or, rather, the Cult of Hemingway, and their soul-killing dogma of "Show Don't Tell." As a reader, I am fed up with nuanced writing. As a reader, I want narrators to tell me where they're at and what they're feeling and what's actually happening with a single crisp sentence, rather than make me sit through a whole enigmatic scene.

Don't even get me started on literary criticism.

*I'd argue literary fiction is much more expansive than* that.

Literary writers begrudge the public for preferring airport fiction like Nicholas Sparks and Michael Crichton to "serious" writers. But *of course* that's what people read: for the average reader, if you have to sacrifice either great writing or great storytelling, you're going to sacrifice the writing. Who cares whether the book is riddled with adverbs, if the writer knows how to tell a story? The last thing you want to read after working all day at the office or the plant is three hundred beautifully written pages about the overly subtle complexities of some fictional family.

*So you aspire to great storytelling, as opposed to great writing?*

No, I'm greedy. I want both. But that hardly ever happens. That's like wanting to become a musician who's both a good songwriter *and* a good lyricist—in other words, to become Dylan. Instead you usually end up becoming either Lady Gaga or Tom Waits.

*Can I get you started on literary criticism?*

I loathe literary criticism. It's intentionally—sometimes unintentionally—unintelligible. Nobody reads literary criticism who doesn't have or isn't in the midst of trying to acquire an English literature degree. Because it's inaccessible. And because—and this seems, to me, especially unforgivable—it's completely irrelevant to the actual everyday lives of twenty-first-century Americans.

Literary theorists should write as if they were having an actual conversation. To write how they actually speak. Like Plato's dialogues.

*I hate to tell you this, but I think that* is *how they speak.*

Then a limit should be placed on how many "posit"s they're allowed to use per sentence.

Why are they always positing everything? Do you know?

*Other writers have labeled your fiction "vulgar," "profane," "galling," "ignorant," "immature," "misguided," and—incredibly frequently—"vandalism."*

When you're lonely, when you're an outcast, when nobody respects you, sometimes that leaves you wanting to graffiti the Hokages.

*"Hokages"?*

I had *nothing* except that can of paint.

*Are you at work on anything new, besides alter egos?*

Lately I've been collaborating with a pair of physicists at the University of Alabama, Paul French and Ernest Malley, working with art beyond the human sensory experience. Together we make "infrared art"—manipulating the temperature of a surface to create an image, while wearing thermal goggles—and "ultrasonic art"—composing inaudible melodies, using tones far far far below the human hearing range.

*Speaking of "inaccessible," that sounds like the epitome of elitism: art that absolutely no one can comprehend or understand.*

In a sense, maybe. But isn't what's really "elitist" assuming that art for humans is the only art worth making? French and I installed some of our infrared art on the roof of Morgan Hall, and within days we had opossums. A passel, I think, is what a group of opossums is called. We had a passel of opossums on the roof. They loved our piece. We had to dismantle it before they started building burrows up there.

And the bats go totally berserk for our ultrasonic art. Malley and I like to stand out in his yard by his barn and play our ultrasonic hit "Doubled Flowering": the bats will come winging out of the pines, diving from the rafters of the barn, wheeling through the moonlight above us, as Malley's children watch from the kitchen window, terrified. Malley likes to live out his Bruce Wayne fantasies that way. Although French agrees that *I'm* Bruce Wayne, and Malley's our Dick Grayson. French is our Alfred: "Batman's batman." Keeps us out of trouble.

*You've written over a dozen books. Why, now, art "beyond the human sensory experience"?*

Avatar. Yes, *Avatar* is derivative of *FernGully*, and *Dances with Wolves*, and *Nausicaä of the Valley of the Wind*. The story itself isn't unique. But, visually, that world was *breathtaking*. I saw the film in IMAX, in 3D, and honestly was moved to tears. I'd never heard an audience react that way to a movie. People were audibly gasping. Hands were being held by people who obviously were not even somewhat romantically involved.

*Avatar* was in theaters for over seven months, in some cities. Some people were seeing the film every week. And did you hear what happened when it went out of theaters? Support groups formed, all over the country. People were seriously distraught. Some admitted they missed being in that world so much that they had even contemplated suicide.

Scott McCloud saw this coming, though. He has this quote: "At the first sign of a technology that can deliver vivid, uncompromising immersion, few will be able to resist its spell. Many may even trade in the world they're given at birth for the new worlds that technology and imagination will combine to create. Virtual Reality is the final destination for the collective journey taken by storytellers throughout history—the journey toward the creation of a world so real it can make us forget the one we live in."

I'm terrified of where we're headed. Take something like *World of Warcraft*, an MMORPG with millions of addicts. That game's already killed people. In China alone, a number of people have died after staying awake two, three, four days to play the game. And now imagine if that world weren't 2D. Imagine if that world were 3D, like *Avatar*. If VRMMORPGs like *The World R:X* or *Aincrad* actually existed. If Oculus Rift ever hits the market.

I'm not worried about climate change, flu epidemics, wars over water. It's story's power that terrifies me.

*Hereafter—*

We're missing the dancing. This has to be the last question. And I'm not going to answer unless you're wearing your mask.

...

Thanks. Perfect. Now that you're ready, I'm ready.

Actually, I already know what I want to talk about. I want to talk about Heather Sellers. Sellers has written a number of books about creative writing that I use when I'm teaching: *Page After Page, Chapter After Chapter*. Anyway, did you know that she has prosopagnosia?

*What?*

Prosopagnosia. Or "face blindness." Aimee Bender published a story in *The Paris Review* recently narrated by a kid with prosopagnosia. Anyway, Sellers actually has it. She can't distinguish between faces. She can recognize people, but she has to rely on other characteristics: body shape, hair color, gait, pitch of voice. Sellers didn't even realize that she had it, that she was any different, until she was forty. I had never heard of it before she was diagnosed. After she told me, I always wanted to write a story about prosopagnosia, but Bender beat me to it. I'm still bitter, but I can only blame myself. I had the premise, but, like Borges, I got lazy. I didn't even manage to write a story about the story. Borges at least would have done that.

Jane Goodall also suffers from prosopagnosia. Which fascinates me, and here's why. A woman who can't recognize human faces spends her entire adult life living with apes? And not only living with, but—and this was controversial, because you aren't supposed to do this, you're supposed to *number* your subjects—not only living with, but *naming* the apes? Breaking fundamental laws of the field experiment in order to make some sort of connection? In some ways, Jane Goodall's may be the saddest story in the history of the world.

But that can be the reader's condition, too: face blindness. *Kiss of the Spider Woman*, "Brief Interviews with Hideous Men," "Edgemont Drive," those stories are composed entirely of dialogue, and not only that, but attach *no names*. The only way to identify who's speaking which line is by the content of what's being said; the only way to learn what a character looks like is by what the characters say.

And that's Sellers. She wouldn't know I have wrinkles at the corners of my eyes unless we were standing there in front of her and you said, "Like those wrinkles near Michael's eyes."

*What would she see, looking at you? Just a blurry face?*

No no no, she still sees a face. Like when you look at the face of a bird. A crow, let's say. When you look at a crow's face, is it blurry?

*No, it's just a crow's face.*

Now let's say I were to show you photographs of seven different crows, with only their faces. Could you tell the crows apart?

*Probably not.*

Because to you, when you look at a crow's face, "it's just a crow's face." To you, those faces are all the same. If you were put in a situation where you *had* to distinguish between different crows, you would use other features—size, bent wingtips, discolored feathers—to tell the crows apart.

Well, for Sellers, our faces "are just human faces." But that weakness has also strengthened her other abilities. Like with this interview, for example: how will the reader recognize me as Michael Martone? The title might say that's who I am, but how will they actually *know?* They won't. I could be anyone. I could be you, pretending to be me.

But Sellers would know. Let's say you paraphrased something: inserted an "anyhow" for an "anyway," for example. I always say anyway, never anyhow, because anyhow sounds snobby. So let's say when you were transcribing our conversation you swapped an anyhow for one of my anyways. Well, Sellers would catch it. She would recognize that this Michael Martone you were quoting in your interview wasn't actually Michael Martone. And that's because she knows my speech patterns—knows my speech patterns so well that she can recognize me when she sees me even though to her my face *is just a human face.*

*You just named Jane Goodall's "the saddest story in the history of the world," but in "The Giants of Cardiff" you dubbed some plaque "the saddest thing in the history of the world."*

In "The Giants of Cardiff" I was writing about the Pioneer plaque. That's not just "some plaque." Do you remember the Pioneer plaque? You were born when? What, 1991, 1992, 1993?

*1987.*

You look very young. Any*way*, the Pioneer plaque was a gold plate attached to the Pioneer spacecraft. The plaque was a pictorial message: hoping the spacecraft might be intercepted by extraterrestrials, the scientists designed a pictogram the extraterrestrials could use to calculate the origin of the spacecraft. It was a map. It was meant to lead them back to us. When I was a kid, I was obsessed with NASA. I had a poster of the Pioneer plaque on my bedroom ceiling. It's what I woke to every morning.

The map was designed using a number of symbols: along the top was a diagram of a hydrogen atom; in the middle a radial pattern showed our sun's position to the center of our galaxy; at the bottom of the plaque were images of the nine planets of our solar system, with each identified by binary numbers giving that planet's approximate distance from the sun.

But the sad thing, the saddest thing in the history of the world, is off to the side: the scientists included images of us, our species, on the plaque. A naked man standing alongside a naked woman. And the man is waving—at, supposedly, the extraterrestrials who would find him. It's an expression of goodwill: the man is a two-dimensional nude diplomat. And what's so sad is the look on this man's face. He's so *happy* to meet the extraterrestrials. Like a boy on a playground making his very first friend.

He's the ultimate expression of our loneliness as a species. It's lonely for us, on this planet, being here with only ourselves. We would give anything for another sentient species to exist, some other species we could communicate with. We just want someone to talk to. But there's nobody out there. The Pioneer plaque is a postcard we sent to our imaginary friends.

Our writing is a product of that loneliness. And in the end we're still only talking to ourselves.

# AN INTERVIEW WITH MICHAEL MARTONE

Michael Martone speaks quickly, gestures constantly, and often makes himself smile. When we met, he had wavy silver hair, streaked with black, which he had sworn not to cut until President George W. Bush was "impeached." His essays are playful: in "How to Hide a Tank: Camouflage, Realism, and Believing Our Eyes," he hints, "I wrote this lecture for several reasons; nine of them are secret." His stories are intricate: in "I Love a Parade," he speaks of having developed a fascination with writers whose stories "telescoped stories within stories to the seventh degree." He has championed "the aesthetic of the TV dinner, the pre-cooked and flash-frozen, the heat and serve, the shake and bake, the poppin' fresh."

We met for lunch at a brewery on the coast of Lake Michigan, splitting a pesto pizza in a narrow booth across from a titanic copper tank, for fermentation, where a bearded brewer was flipping levers and studying dials. Martone brought a friend, "V," a local English professor with cropped reddish hair and a catching laugh, who asked if she could sit in on the interview. Some of the following questions are hers—she occasionally interrupted with a question of her own, when something interested her—but she asked that those remain unmarked. One question was suggested by something the bearded brewer shouted to a bartender, but it was, again, V who asked the question.

As the interview concluded—I still had a few questions, but V was paying the bill, and Martone was late for a visit to a creative writing workshop—Martone said, "Is that enough? If you want more, you can just make stuff up. Really. It's your interview. We didn't even talk about the interview as a form, but the interview is a relatively recent form, with *The Paris Review* interviews being the ones that sort of got it going. But why shouldn't you do something different with the interview, instead of just Q and A, Q and A, Q and A?"

After leaving the brewery, I followed Martone to the creative writing workshop, where he had volunteered to give a Q&A. Eleven students were enrolled in the workshop, although two were absent. The others—many with flushed cheeks from their trek across the snowy campus—seemed shy, but quickly warmed to Martone. I should note that some of their questions, and his answers, are included among the questions below. Like mine, and V's, their questions will be treated simply as belonging to the "interviewer."

■ ■ ■
■ □ ■
■ □ ■

*For* Townships, *you chose Ohio, Indiana, Michigan, Illinois, Wisconsin, Minnesota, and Iowa to represent the Midwest. But you have also said you adore the fluidity of the Midwest, how "as a physical region we haven't agreed where it is." What makes the Midwest so hard to define?*

The Midwest has no distinctive geological features. It's not like the Mountain West or the Pacific Coast or the Mid-Atlantic. It's not like the South: the South seceded from the Union, so the South is easy to define. But the Midwest doesn't have a geological feature or a history that will mark out its region. As the country settled west, it blew through this part of the country really quickly. It was only held up briefly by the Civil War. The frontier—cowboy stories and things like that—wasn't here long enough to give it an identity.

So in *Townships* I argue that the one thing that maybe marks the Midwest is the township grid. If you're flying over the country and you look down, you know you're over the Midwest if you can see the grid: you see it in the fields, in the road system. Even though all the other states are in township grids—Alaska, Hawaii, all of them except for the original thirteen colonies—it's only in the Midwestern states that you can actually *see the grid from above.*

But that's only a manmade physical feature, a Jeffersonian imposition on the landscape. So although the grid can be used to define the Midwest, I think it also adds to the notion of the Midwest as a kind of strange, imaginary place. Since no one really knows where it is, the Midwest has to define itself.

*So the Midwest lacks a sense of identity?*

Absolutely. I chose Ohio, Indiana, Michigan, Illinois, Wisconsin, Minnesota, and Iowa, but some Midwesterners will give you a whole other group of states. Iowans will say the Midwest is Nebraska, North and South Dakota, Kansas, and Oklahoma. And you'll say, "No way—that's the Plains." Or you'll ask Nebraskans, "Where's Ohio?" and they'll say, "That's in the East." But nobody in Ohio will say Ohio is in the East.

One quality of the Midwest is that the people who actually live there and are quite proud of it don't know where it is. If you live in Alabama, you know you're Southern. But the Midwesterners have no idea. So they have to make it up on their own. And because of that, they don't think the Midwest is important. When I say that I write about Indiana, people in Indiana say, "Why?" But if one of my students in Alabama says, "I'm going to write about Alabama," the rest of the students say, "Well, what kept you? Of course you'd write about Alabama."

The key to understanding the Midwest and the Midwesterner is that, if you grew up here, if you live here, if you call yourself a Midwesterner, you secretly feel like you're what's holding this country together. It's a secret pride. We don't want to talk about it, but we're really what America is. We're the heartland. We're holding the dens of iniquity, California and New York, onto this continent. Without us, they would be nothing. That's what we secretly believe. But at the same time, we think that we're in the middle of nowhere. So there's this weird drama in the Midwest: simultaneously feeling very very important and very very marginalized. You're in the middle of everything and the middle of nowhere.

*In the forward to* Pink Houses and Family Taverns *you wrote about a trip your parents made to visit you in Tuscaloosa: strangers would stop at your house when they saw the Indiana license plates and introduce themselves because they were from Indiana too.*

This isn't just an Indiana thing. I was at a lighthouse museum or ship museum or something in the Upper Peninsula of Michigan and I had my car with Alabama plates, and when we came out of the museum there was a note under our windshield wipers that said, "Oh, you're from Alabama too." So it's not that it doesn't happen to other people in other places. But I think Indiana is special. They say Indiana is the crossroads of America, which is a nice public relations model, but it's also true. You have to go through Indiana whether you're going west or going north. It's this nexus. And so Indiana is a contradiction: it's sweet home Indiana, but it's also an incredibly fluid state. There are sweeping migrations of people that come through it.

The next book I'm going to publish is called *Racing in Place*. It's about this kind of frenetic motion and also this kind of staticness in the Midwest. People move out and people come back and there are always people moving through it. All that energy creates a kind of static. The Indianapolis 500 is symbolic of that. The region is about five hundred miles in any direction from Indianapolis. But the drivers go in a circle. Two hundred times. Very fast. Racing in place.

*Your work often examines these cultural icons of Indiana.*

That was a big discovery for me, that I could write about Indiana. I was in a little liberal arts college in the middle of Indiana University. I was in this really cool dorm. We thought we were really cool. A lot of black, a lot of berets, cafés. And we had readings. We were all disaffected and completely jaded and smoked clove cigarettes. And we were writing all of these bad copies of things, which is what you do anyway. One day I discovered that the hero of the football team, a guy named Harry Gonso—honest, that's his name—if you're from Ohio or Michigan, you know about football, but Indiana is not about football, it's about basketball, but this one team was the Cinderella team, the only time Indiana University ever had a winning football team, and it went all the way, and the guy's name was Harry Gonso, and he was a hero in Indiana, and I found out he had lived in my dorm. So here we are, all sitting around, being beatniky, and writing about feeling upset about World War I. And I wrote this little poem about Harry Gonso, and I could see that all of these kids were really interested. That was an interesting lesson: the fact that Harry Gonso had been in their dorm still meant something to them.

Then when I went to graduate school in Maryland, the first time I was ever out of Indiana, all of my colleagues were from eastern schools, and they knew more about India than they did about Indiana, and I was still writing my little modernist stories about these big cities and European wars, being very existential. And then we would go to the bar afterward and I'd say, "You know, when I was growing up, Fort Wayne was seventh on Hitler's list." And these kids were like, "Wow. That's interesting." I was like, "It is? It seems completely boring to me."

*In "Appliances: Domestic Detail and Describing Rituals of the Ordinary" you wrote that you always picture the interior of your childhood home in Fort Wayne when you read a story, that "it is the house in which for [you] all stories begin." Are there other ways your childhood influences your reading and writing?*

I was read to a lot. As a kid I would go to my mom's high school English class, where she read *The Odyssey* over and over again. But another thing that was really influential was this guy who used to be on television called Captain Kangaroo. Captain Kangaroo would read books. The illustrations for that generation of books were wonderful: *Make Way for Ducklings*, *Curious George*, those types of books from the '30s and '40s. And the television program would show the pictures, but they would have to animate them. They couldn't animate them by drawing regular animation pictures, so they used the camera to move around, or pan, or cut to various pictures. I loved that as a kid, watching some of the books that my mom read to me come to life—even though, again, they weren't actually moving.

I have an interest in television because—do you know who invented television? Philo T. Farnsworth. Honest, his name was Philo T. Farnsworth. He was from Utah, but guess where he ended up.

*…Indiana.*

Not just Indiana. Fort Wayne, Indiana! He invented the electron scanning ray tube that was first used for television. It was the first invention that RCA didn't invent, so RCA claimed that they invented it. Then he was in court for a long time. Finally RCA lost and had to pay him for his invention, the television, but by that time he was broke. He went to Fort Wayne to start his own factory, but of course none of us have ever had a Farnsworth television, so it sort of died out. He ended up a kind of broken and insane man in his basement trying to create fusion. His house was actually right across from the insane asylum in Fort Wayne.

The only time Farnsworth was ever on television was on a reality show: *To Tell the Truth*. You know that game show? It's an old '50s game show. Three people come out, and a little story is told about you. In this case, "Philo T. Farnsworth invented the television." Then a guy comes out and says, "My name is Philo T. Farnsworth." Then the next guy comes out, "My name is Philo T. Farnsworth." Next guy says, "My name is Philo T. Farnsworth." Then the host asks questions and tries to guess which one is the real Philo T. Farnsworth. It turns out that they didn't guess right, so Philo T. Farnsworth got fifty bucks and a carton of cigarettes.

*I know you were influenced by Greek mythology, in part because of Edith Hamilton, a native of Fort Wayne, and her book* Mythology. *What other stories have influenced your writing?*

A great story, one I think about often and write about a lot, is a story written by William Gass called "In the Heart of the Heart of the Country." It's not really a story: it's more of a fiction. The narrator, a philosophy teacher at Purdue, has broken up with his girlfriend, one of his students. And because he's heartbroken, he goes to this small town in Indiana called "B" to escape and think about love. There are thirty-six sections. Just sitting around thinking about this town and being heartbroken. I read it in college and thought it was amazing. First, it's set in Indiana. Second, *nothing happens.* There's just the gorgeousness of the language and the collageness of it.

*Jerome Stern says that "artists tend to be an unruly bunch—no sooner do they learn their craft than they stretch the boundaries, test their limits, find out what is really true." Your work often seems to topple these boundaries.* Michael Martone *is a collection of fictional contributor's notes;* The Blue Guide to Indiana *is a fictional travel guide, sections of which were published as nonfiction in newspapers and magazines; and some of your stories and essays, such as "Trying: An Introduction to Introduction: Four Found Introductions," are composed almost entirely of excerpts lifted from other texts.*

That's the artist's job, to do that kind of boundary work. In some ways you can think of the writer as a trickster figure.

*You've called the writer a "counterfeiter and liar, manipulator of texts and voice, stealer of experience."*

Or think of the writer as Hermes from Greek mythology, who is both the messenger of business and commerce and the patron of thieves. That's the role I like to play with. I'm not really sure where the boundaries are, but I'm constantly jumping back and forth, and the jumping helps to make those boundaries clear.

*You've taken your experiments with those boundaries even beyond writing and into your own life. In college you and your friends enrolled a fake student, John Smith, and even attended his classes. How did that experiment start?*

Well. Probably drunkenly. But then that's what being drunk is. It's about transcendence. When you go to a concert, the music is played so loud that you can't hear it. And that's why you go. You want the sound of it, the actual vibration of it, to take you somewhere. It's the same as Edgar Allan Poe. Students don't get Edgar Allan Poe. They don't understand that what Edgar Allan Poe actually wanted to do was arrange words in such a way that it would act like alcohol, that it would act like drugs, that it would stone you. Students read a poem like "The Bells" where he's going "the bells, bells, bells, bells," and they think, "Well this is stupid." But his desire was to break that boundary.

That's why college students do those kinds of pranks. They might not be conscious of it, but they're doing exactly what art does, testing those boundaries and trying to move beyond them. Even the act of getting drunk is an act of trying to escape the categories that keep you in a certain place. I love the Talking Heads song where years later he wakes up and says, "How did I get here? This is not my beautiful wife. This is not my beautiful home." That's the way life is. What art does, and what college is meant to do, is to say, "Wait a minute, I'm not going to settle into these things without at least examining what they are." Nothing is normal.

One way to think about art is as framed deviance. That's an Aristotelian idea. Aristotle thought it was incredibly important for us to experience emotions and sensations that are beyond the pale. Why do kids love horror movies? Because it's framed, it's a theater: people are not actually having their heads decapitated by chainsaws. But you can experience it, and maybe find something in that experience worthwhile—the expression of that emotion, or the fact that you have that emotional violence within you. You want to express it in some way, but in a way that's safe and controlled.

*John Smith has his own address now, and even receives alumni mail. So in some ways he's crossed that boundary between fiction and nonfiction.*

I have this friend who studies the geography of fictional places. People like the fictional places so much that they begin to appear in the real world. Hawthorne wrote "The House of the Seven Gables," and now you can visit the House of the Seven Gables in Salem, Massachusetts. It's almost as if a fictional thing can come into being even more easily than a nonfictional thing.

Borges has stories like this. Borges doesn't really write stories: he calls them fictions. They're usually essays written by fictional people. He has one called "The Theme of the Traitor and the Hero," and in it there's this researcher writing the history of his ancestor who was a famous hero. And the researcher discovers his ancestor had been assassinated, and it turns out that he was assassinated in a theatre just like Lincoln, and he uttered some words that were actually from Julius Caesar. So the essay writer says, "It's weird enough to think that history repeats itself, but it's really strange if history repeats literature." In the end it turns out that the traitor was this hero in the midst of the revolution. He was found out, proof was given, so he said, "I only have one request, and that is, when you kill me, you do so in such a way that it makes me a hero and helps the revolution." So the writer of this history is confronted with whether or not he should expose the truth. This is from the book by Borges called *Labyrinths*—it's all about truth, history, fact, fiction. Again, it's as if these fictional things, once they're made, become more real. It's like making robots and winding them up and then they're in your life.

*You've published poems under the name Neal Bowers, which was also the name of a poet who had written a book about his hunt for someone who had plagiarized his poems.*

Again, that was about pointing out the thin ice we're all on, that the author is not static, that even Neal Bowers, whoever "he" is, is already a kind of collaboration and creation. Neal Bowers never stole a word from someone else's poem? We've all had the experience of writing something, and you really like it, and then a couple months later you realize, my God, it seemed like me, but this is something I read when I was a *kid!*

Another Borges story is "Pierre Menard, Author of the *Quixote*." In it Pierre Menard writes the *Don Quixote*, word for word, exactly the same as the original *Don Quixote*, but without looking at it. He arranges his life in such a way that when he writes his novel it's exactly the same book. Then he says, "Let me quote from the *Don Quixote*," and he quotes a paragraph. Then he says, "Now let me quote the Pierre Menard." And it's the same paragraph, word for word, but then the critic says, "But notice the subtle nuances." And it's true. If I wrote Beethoven's Fifth Symphony we would never think that it's good in the way Beethoven's Fifth Symphony is. It would be a different piece of music, a piece of music that could have its own delights, its own boringness. Knowing that I wrote it, you would listen to it differently. It exposes the myth that artists are solitary individual geniuses—it's far more collaborative than what we might think it is. We need to examine why we're holding onto that notion of individual geniuses being so special and so worth legal protection.

*Has the other Neal Bowers ever contacted you about your contributions?*
I think he might be mad. I used to work with him, and he always seemed grumpy.

*You've said that you consider "The Moon over Wapakoneta" science fiction regionalism. What other new breeds of fiction do you see evolving in your work?*

Well, the idea of reinvigorating regionalism is one thing. I'm also interested in science fiction that doesn't depend upon the front part of the story, but on the back part. A science fiction in which nothing happens, basically. In *Star Wars*, Luke Skywalker is in the middle of nowhere, but he becomes the hero of the whole universe. I want to write a story about Luke Skywalker who's in the middle of nowhere while the wars are going on. Just farming.

I'm also working on postcards as a genre, exploring what a postcard is, how it collaborates with an artist—often unknown, because one side has a picture—and how it also collaborates with the postal service, because that's the way it's delivered, or "published." I'm doing an interview right now with another writer and we're doing it by postcard. He sends me questions on postcards, I have to answer on postcards, and then he responds on postcards. It takes a lot longer than this.

Another experiment that I've already started is to create fictions where I don't sign my name. That's the next big hurdle for me, to get into literary magazines not using my name. Not even using Neal Bowers's name. So far what I've done is I've made advertisements. In the back of literary magazines there are these little ads called exchange ads. You know, you don't really have any money to buy advertising, and you don't really want to make money advertising, but since you're using folios you have a couple pages left over. So you call up the literary magazine at Michigan State and say, "Do you have an ad? Give us your ad and we'll put it in the back of our magazine and you put our ad in the back your magazine." Well, I wrote ads for made-up companies and services and sent them to literary magazines and asked them to publish them in the ad section without making any reference to the fact that they're fictional.

I'd also like to work on a book of blurbs of books that don't exist. Or that do exist. In some way I'd like to work with the blurb, which I started with *Michael Martone*.

*You had another insight into "The Moon over Wapakoneta" that seems revealing. You wrote that the story "[keeps] the narrator and the reader both in flight and perfectly still." Most of your fiction seems to create that equilibrium, especially* Michael Martone.

They just asked me what I want for the cover of the book *Racing in Place*. I want a blimp. Lots of blimps. I love blimps and zeppelins, these massive ships that do somehow actually move, but relatively slowly. They float, they're lighter than air, and they can move a great deal of merchandise, but in some ways they're not moving. Human clouds.

Maybe that's how the equilibrium developed. Looking up at the sky, looking at clouds. Clouds seem so static. But as you watch them, they change. Or it's like watching a herd of cattle. They're so docile, so bovine. But you look at them, and you turn around—

*And even though they're standing still, you look back, and they're grazing on a different hill.*

A completely different hill. Or what's really great is if they think you're there to feed them. You're looking at them, you turn away, you look back—*and they're right behind you.*

*Reading* Michael Martone *is a* Where's Waldo *experience: there are all these fictional Michael Martones wandering around, riding bicycles, walking dogs, mowing lawns, and even though none of them are real, one of them will be wearing Waldo's striped shirt, and another will be carrying Waldo's cane. Is the real Michael Martone hiding somewhere inside the stories? How much of* Michael Martone *is autobiographical?*

Well, one of the jobs of *Michael Martone* is to make you think, how many Matthews are there? And who is the real Matthew? It also brings up the question, how well can we know who the real Michael Martone is? There are these lies we tell ourselves, these delusions we live under. So to ask me that is to go against the spirit of the book. It's like looking in a mirror and trying to see the back of your head. You try to move fast or something to catch it but you can't. There are certain blind spots you're always going to have about yourself.

*Traditional narratives create a place where characters live, whereas your stories create a place for readers to live in. You talked some about this in* Unconventions, *saying you "liked the idea of a fiction without character or plot, a fiction that provides instead costumes and props for the reader to employ." What attracts you to this sort of storytelling?*

There's a big argument among writers and artists about who controls the meaning of the story. Whose story is it? I have a lot of writer friends who want to hold that idea steady. That's what a workshop is. You go to a workshop and the assumption is that your fellows will help you make your meaning clear. But there's a growing belief that, in fact, that's not the way art works—any art, not just stories. The meaning, or what a story is, is often up to the way that the reader, who we usually think of as a passive receptor, uses the story. When you watch television, you watch it with the remote control, and you're clicking around to various things, participating in the making of a narrative that the people at NBC didn't know about: they didn't know you were going to be watching *Friends* and a *Law and Order* rerun at the same time. So it isn't so much a preference for that kind of storytelling—it's just recognizing that's the way people always were. What attracted me as a reader were the kind of stories like the William Gass story, stories that I participated in, where I could jump around, go back and read it. Sometimes I read that story and there are thirty-six sections, and other times when I read it I think he's published it without a couple sections, or he's added another section. It's never the same twice. So when I write stories, I write stories where I'm conscious of that. I think of myself more as an arranger as opposed to a composer. I take music that's already there and arrange it in a new way, so the reader can participate in the actual playing of the music.

*What are your workshops like, then?*

I like to play this game called Molly and Ned. The name of the game is Molly and Ned, the object of the game is to guess the rules of the game, and I can only answer your questions with yes or no.

I won't actually make you play it. We'll cut to the chase. I use this game when we're talking about getting caught up in routines, about getting caught in a static worldview. The one thing you take for granted, as a writer, is your language. As soon as you were two years old you were saying, "Hello, can I have a glass of water?" And now here you are years later wanting to be an artist that uses language, and you're still thinking about language in that same way. Unless I point it out to you, all of us would say pretty much the same thing: *I'd like a drink. I'd like some water. Would you give me a drink? I'm thirsty.* The way we use language is pretty much content driven. But if you're writing, all of those sentences are different. How does a fish know that it's in water? You take it out of water. The water you're in is your language. You're so far in it that you can't see it until I take you out of it. That's what Molly and Ned does.

The name of the game is Molly and Ned, the object of the game is to guess the rules of the game, and I can answer questions yes or no. When we play, students make an assumption when they ask questions. Their questions have informational content and they assume they're going to get some sort of information when I answer yes or no. "Can you get points?" "Does the game have an end?" "Is there a winner?" I answer: no, yes, no. These are the kind of questions they ask. No one questions truth. It takes a while for students to realize that I'm giving contradictory answers.

Here's the trick. All I do is listen for the first letter of the last word in the sentence. If it's M (Molly) or before, I answer yes. If it's N (Ned) or after, I answer no. It takes about an hour, with a lot of coaching, for people to actually see that. Even after I say I'm not telling the truth, even after I tell them they're not going to get a direct answer from me, people keep asking, "Well, can five people play the game?" Yes. "Can five people play?" No. It's incredibly frustrating. On my student evaluations at the end of the year, everyone always hates Molly and Ned. They think it's a waste of an hour. But they always put it on my evaluations. They've always remembered that game.

There's a story about Hemingway and the Rorschach test. The Rorschach is a projective test. They show you an inkblot and then they ask, "What do you see in the picture?" And they write down everything you say, and you see a butterfly, two people kissing. But they're also paying attention to how many responses you have. The average response to each inkblot is about eight. But Ernest Hemingway had four times as many responses. Now, you could say that it's because he's Ernest Hemingway: he's a genius, he's an artist, he could just see more in each inkblot. But that's not why he could see four times as many. Do you know what he did? He took it. He reached out, and he took the inkblot, and *he turned it.*

Remember what the instructions were? "Tell me what you see in this picture." They don't say, "Don't touch the picture." But most people won't touch

the picture. It's like Molly and Ned. It's what's *not* being said that you have to be aware of, in order to break out of the patterns, the habits, the frame.
*Like mapping boundaries through that "jumping."*

There's another thing I do, a revision thing. Do you have to do revisions? I hate revisions.

What I have students do is write a story, read the story, then put it in a drawer and never look at it again. For a while. Then you start your revision, and all you have to do is rewrite the story as it's already written. Don't try to make it better, because that's the hard part of revision, when you sit down to write a revision and you think you're going to make it a better story. Well, this time you're not going to make it a better story. All I'm asking you to do is to make it exactly the same. But you can't look at it. You have to do it completely from memory. Now, that never happens. At the end of the exercise you have an interesting thing. You have two eight-page stories that are supposed to be the same. Now you can look at those two and say, "Why did I think this was what I wrote? When in fact this is what I wrote?" And what does that tell you? It gets at that whole problem of writing: I have this great idea for a story, and it's in my head, and I've got to get it out of my head and onto a piece of paper. That's where it always breaks down.

You know what they call a landing on an aircraft carrier? One of the hardest things human beings have devised to do is to take a fourteen-million-dollar airplane and land it on a landing strip floating in the middle of the ocean going forty knots into the wind at night. It's incredibly difficult to do. And they have workshops. There's a guy on the deck who's directing the airplane in, and the landing itself is videotaped, and when they land the airplane they go downstairs and they show them the videotapes and say, "Well." Nobody ever lands the airplane perfectly. So what they call it is a "controlled crash."

That's the way I think of stories and writing. It's never going to be perfect. The key thing is, that fourteen-million-dollar airplane, you landed it: you can get back in it and fly again. It wasn't pretty, but you landed it, and that's good enough. You should feel really good about that. So you get in the airplane, you fly around, and you try again. So that's the way I think of revision, or stories, all stories. A controlled crash.

Often what happens to writers is they think, "I'm going to write my great opus, I'm going to write it, actually finish it, then try to publish it." No, instead: fast, cheap, and out of control. Look at Jasper Johns. How many flags did he paint? Enough with the flags already! But no, you just keep working on something, working on something. Some of them are okay, some of them are failures. But each time, again, crash landing on that aircraft carrier. Get back in that airplane, and get going.

# AN INTERVIEW WITH MICHAEL MARTONE

In 2009, Michael Martone began publishing a series of interviews. Each interview was published under the pen name Matt Baker, each interview was titled "An Interview with Michael Martone," and each interview was with himself, Michael Martone. For each interview, Martone wrote Matt Baker's questions, then wrote Michael Martone's answers to those questions. Martone then published these interviews—some as "nonfiction," most as simply "interviews"—in literary magazines ranging from *Meridian* to *Ninth Letter* to *Southern Indiana Review*. In each magazine, the contributor's note for the "interviewer" read: "Matt Baker was born in Fort Smith, Arkansas, and now works as an editor for *Oxford American*."

My name is Matt Baker. I was born in Fort Smith, Arkansas. In 2009, I was working as an editor for *Oxford American*.

Martone has since admitted he chose to appropriate my identity for his "interviewer" while trolling through online literary magazines: when he spotted my picture on *Oxford American*'s website, he "saw a bit of [himself] in [me]" and "right away, thought, 'Michael, that's your man.'" Martone did not ask my permission—neither before writing, nor before publishing the interviews. I did not realize I had been "interviewing" Martone until the eighth interview was published: a friend sent me a link to *Devil's Lake*'s "An Interview with Michael Martone," which featured, alongside the interview, photos both of Martone and of me—Martone had taken a photo of me from Facebook (I've since changed my privacy settings) and had given the photo to *Devil's Lake*. Things did get worse from there. As I actually read that interview, and later the others, I discovered Martone not only had stolen my name, and my photo, but also even from my stories: the interviews themselves included phrases, sentences, sometimes entire paragraphs lifted from the few stories I had published in magazines.

I was a fan of Martone's work—I had read both *Michael Martone* and *Dou-*

*ble-Wide*—and so, rather than seeking legal recourse, I took a bus from Arkansas to Tuscaloosa, took a taxi from the station to Martone's house (I'm equally adept at internet stalking—finding Martone's address took mere minutes of googling), approached Martone where he was hunched over weeding some flowers in his yard, and asked him if I could interview him—actually interview him—here now at his house.

So, after Martone had taken off his work gloves and gardening hat and agreed to be interviewed, and after his wife had come out onto the porch and seen his pile of uprooted plants and shrieked and then chased him away from her flower beds (the "weeds" Martone had been weeding were actually white flowers; "I've never seen such weedy flowers, before—I really thought that they were weeds," Martone said), and after Martone had scrubbed the dirt from his hands and wiped the sweat from his face and poured some coffee into a pair of cracked mugs and taken me into his study, a room furnished with velvet curtains and leather armchairs and a claw-footed desk and wooden bookcases, their shelves crammed with various mementos—a dream catcher, antique perfume bottles, a tin robot, a ceramic dinosaur, superhero figurines, a reproduction of a painting of Dorian Gray, a framed illustration of Plato's cave, Yoshimoto Cubes, Sonobe origami, twenty-sided dice, piles of golden stickers, stacks of stamped postcards, a rumpled ghillie suit—I, Matt Baker, asked Michael Martone some questions. This, what follows, is what he had to say for himself.

☐ ☐ ☐
☐ ☐ ☐
☐ ☐ ☐

*You've published eight separate interviews using my name.*

That count may actually be somewhat low.

*In many of "my" interviews, you mention your friend Paul French: in one, French is founder of a band called AVALANCHE that performs only cover songs by fictional bands; in another, French is an expat poet living in Kyoto; in another, French is a physicist who collaborates with you on infrared and ultrasonic "art" installments here in Tuscaloosa.*

    *But, of course, Paul French does not exist.*

It's not that Paul doesn't exist—

*Would it have been more accurate to say, instead, that Paul French was a pen name used by Isaac Asimov for his Lucky Starr novels, a pen name later appropriated by you and used in "my" interviews as a synonym for Michael Martone? That the Paul Frenches in "my" interviews are actually placeholders, are actually you, Michael Martone?*

Yes, there it is. Before going to Johns Hopkins—before I became a writer of fictions—I lived in Kyoto for several years as a poet. And AVALANCHE is my band: I'm the vocalist, and also the drummer, on AVALANCHE's three albums. Have you heard our latest album, *Kaonashi*? I have it here on vinyl. We can listen to it, if you like.

*In another of "my" interviews, you said, "Paul wrote a novel called* Planetarium, *which he self-published in a shed on his parents' farm just outside of Fort Wayne. Each page of* Planetarium *is nailed to the walls or the windows of this rickety toolshed. These pages aren't numbered—aren't ordered in any way. But they wallpaper the walls, plaster the windows, hang from the rafters." Does the shed exist?*

The shed exists. On, of course, my parents' farm. It's still there today: each year I use my research budget here at the University of Alabama to send our first-year MFAs to Fort Wayne on a chartered bus. A few at a time, they go into the shed. Then after they've read the book they head into the house to try some of my mother's goat milk ice cream. The MFAs always rave about the ice cream, but never have much to say about the shed. My parents' farm is on 1050 N, between 450 E and 500 E—in Fort Wayne, the roads are numbered, like the pages of a book.

*But unlike the pages of* Planetarium. *Why publish* Planetarium *in a shed? As opposed to other books with unnumbered pages, like* Composition No. 1, *Marc Saporta's boxed novel?*

Having the pages in a box wouldn't be the same. Even hanging the pages from a wall in some museum. My concept, for *Planetarium*, came from arcade games. Do you remember arcade games? This was in the '80s, so maybe you were too young. Arcade games were these machines the size of a closet. For playing video games. But, on each machine, you only could play one game. Maybe you didn't see, but we have a Wii downstairs. A console like that's like a turntable: any record I own, I can put it in my turntable and play it; any video game I own, I can put it in my console and play it. But arcade games were more like a jukebox—a jukebox with one song. You would put in your quarter, but you could play only that one game: *Asteroids, Pac-Man, Tron*—

*I thought* Tron *was a fictional arcade game—from the film* Tron.

The arcade game was fictional when *Tron* the film was released, but afterward became nonfictional. *Tron* the arcade game crossed over, from fiction to nonfiction—the same way fictional words in novels sometimes will cross over, become nonfictional, actually enter the English language. "Chortled," for instance, from *Through the Looking-Glass*.

In "your" interviews, of course, you were crossing over in the other direction—from the nonfictional you, at home in your apartment in Arkansas, to the fictional you I put onto the page.

You wouldn't always stand at an arcade game, though. Some—*Sinistar, After Burner, Senjō no Kizuna*—you'd actually have to *climb in*. To play *After Burner*—to "read" its story—you had to climb in, sit in the cockpit, and grab the joystick. Your floor was its floor, your ceiling its ceiling. That was part of the story: being there, in that room.

That was the idea behind *Planetarium*. To write a story the reader would have to *walk into*. To *be inside of*. A story that could become, briefly, the reader's ceiling and walls and floor. The reader's entire world. But that wasn't just a gimmick: the idea was tied to the content of the story. What made that story *possible*.

*Have you written any "building fictions" since?*

In 2009 a gallery in Chelsea hosted an exhibit by Yayoi Kusama. Kusama's work has always fascinated me—*Cosmic Space (TWBBAA)* especially, and *Self Portrait*—so that semester when I was in Brooklyn visiting my friend Neal, he took me into town to see the exhibit.

Kusama had built one piece for the exhibit itself: *Aftermath of Obliteration of Eternity*, what the gallery's curators were billing an "infinity room." This certain room in the gallery was empty—white ceiling, white walls, gray floor—

except for what looked like a small house. The house was white, too, with one door, a single metal handle. The house was *Aftermath of Obliteration of Eternity*. Dozens of people were in line, and even as we got into line, more people were stepping in behind us. A curator, dressed in a black suit and a black dress shirt, stood at the door with a metal pocket watch: each group was allowed to enter the piece for only ninety seconds, to keep the line moving. And if that curator hadn't been there, the line wouldn't have moved period. Nobody would have ever come out. It was sort of the arts equivalent of Incandenza's *Infinite Jest (IV) / Infinite Jest (V)*. "Where is the beginning of the end that comes at the end of the beginning?"

Kusama, incidentally, is mesmerizing in person. In the '90s, in Italy, she sculpted a series of pumpkins, bright yellow with black polka dots, and then at the exhibit presided over the pumpkins wearing a cape and hat—that same bright yellow, same black polka dots—with this elegant crypsis. She also sculpted these tentacles once and then—

*What was in the "infinity room"? At the gallery?*

You step into the room, and the curator shuts the door. You're in a room made of mirrors, standing on a slab of black stone, in the dark. It's not lit: you can't see your own body, let alone Neal's standing there with you. What you can see are golden lights. Golden lights shaped like cylinders. You know where Neal is only because of his outline: you can't see his actual body, only where the shape of his body blocks the lights. The surface of the mirrors is black, and the lights reflect there, wall to wall, mirror to mirror, seem to be hanging in the distance—some just beyond reach, some neighborhoods away, beyond where the actual walls of the "infinity room" are, beyond where the actual walls of the gallery are, past Chelsea and the Garment District and the Theater District and even the Bronx. But there are no actual lights. You're unsure where the lights are coming from—how many are being reflected in the mirrors, how many are only reflections of reflections—because the actual lights *are not in the room*. Kusama has somehow arranged everything to create the illusion of being in an infinite space with infinite lights, with the actual lights hidden somewhere outside of the room entirely.

I hadn't worked with a "building fiction" since *Planetarium*, but after seeing *Aftermath of Obliteration of Eternity*—after standing there, inside of it, with Neal—I couldn't stop thinking about building another. Kusama didn't need to build a house for *Aftermath of Obliteration of Eternity*: she could have created the same sort of illusion on the wall of the gallery, in a painting or a photograph. But being there inside that 3D piece was a different experience than looking at a 2D piece on the wall—that's what was so dizzying, was being surrounded by it, forgetting yourself in it, the piece becoming your reality.

Ever since, I've been at work on a new "building fiction" project. On the outskirts of Tuscaloosa there's an abandoned elevator factory. Even the teenagers are tired of it—they've already graffitied every window, all of the walls: "I AM THE ANAGRAM," "THIS STARDOM HAS DUNGEONS," "A B C C B A" So I have the factory to myself, when I'm there. Don't mention this to my wife, incidentally—she'd be angry if she knew I was out hopping barbed wire fences, walking hundred-year-old catwalks littered with broken glass. A few weeks ago I tore my jeans on the fence, and I had to tell her it had happened helping Paul French clean out his garage.

*What do you do, in the factory? Are you "publishing" in the factory in the same way as* Planetarium? *Pinning pages to walls?*

No, I wouldn't want to cover up the other text in the factory: what I think of as the "graffiti novel." How I'm publishing—binding the fiction—is much different than how I did in the shed. I shouldn't say anything else. I want readers to experience the fiction without any preconceptions.

*Does the factory have a title?*

The working title is *Tête-à-tête*, but that won't be the actual title. *Tête-à-tête* is just a placeholder.

*What other pen names have you used besides "Matt Baker"?*

I'm glad you asked that. No other interviewer has ever asked me that—not even myself, interviewing myself. And I probably should make some sort of inventory, publicly.

So here's the lineup: fictional interviews, I always publish under your name, Matt Baker. I've published fictional poems under the name Neal Bowers, fictional fiction under the names Alisa Rosenbaum, Eric Blair, William Porter, Samuel Clemens, and Mary Anne Evans, fictional nonfiction under the username zzxyzz [on Wikipedia], fictional advertisements under the name French Co., and fictional songs under the name AVALANCHE.

But that's been a convention in music for decades—a convention since The Beatles. David Byrne, Chris Frantz, Jerry Harrison, and Tina Weymouth weren't expected to publish as "Byrne et al.": they published as Talking Heads. Richard David James doesn't publish as "Richard David James": he publishes as Aphex Twin, Power-Pill, The Dice Man, Polygon Window. Sean John Combs published as Puff Daddy, then P. Diddy, now Diddy. In music, you're expected to have stage names. That's part of the allure—the musicians' personas.

In this country, a musician can earn a living as a musician. Not by selling albums—most don't earn their living from record sales—but by touring. By playing their music live. Musicians don't have to get gigs teaching intro to music courses to undergrad college students—they pay rent with their art. Writers, however, have to get gigs teaching intro to writing courses to undergrad college students—that's the best that they can do, in this country. And that's largely because writers are so uptight. It's not fun to see writers reading work live. Because our writers can't perform. All that our writers know is how to do is string together some metaphors, avoid using adverbs. Our writers can't captivate an audience like storytellers once could. How Lady Gaga can. Our literature here is some of the most unentertaining in the history of our species.

Nobody's paying $90 a seat to see even George Saunders live. Nobody's paying $90 a seat to see Michael Martone. But what if I published as The Thief Vagabond of Dalmatia, and gave readings wearing costumes as whimsical as David Bowie's? What if George Saunders published as Skywriters, and what if Skywriters and The Thief Vagabond of Dalmatia went on tour together, headlining readings opened by local writers? Our shows would be *sellouts*.

*Which meaning of the word?*

My favorite of Asimov's Lucky Starr books was always *Lucky Starr and the Moons of Jupiter*. In the book, Lucky's brother is abducted by aliens from Jupiter and replaced with a look-alike. So Lucky has to go to Sponde, Jupiter's sixty-ninth moon, to try to bring his brother back.

What I loved was this one image: this image of Lucky's ship—after landing on Jupiter, stopping on the way to Sponde—this image of Lucky's ship,

Lucky's face and hands pressed to the glass, Lucky staring quietly at the sixty-nine white and blue and yellow moons hanging there in the sky. Sponde, Atlas, Proteus, Titania—the moons are of various sizes.

And that's how I think of my pen names, my alter egos. I think of readers as being on the planet Jupiter. Sometimes I prefer to be the sun—to send my words to the reader myself—but other times I prefer to bounce my words off of other bodies, off the face of one of the moons.

It colors the light in interesting ways.

*But you've created, not just fictional Matt Bakers and Paul Frenches and Neil Bowerses, but even fictional Michael Martones.*

Yayoi Kusama lives in Tokyo, in, by choice, a mental hospital. Since she was a child, Kusama has had suicidal impulses. I didn't know that until recently, and when I heard it, it made me sad, thinking of her wearing the polka-dotted outfit she'd made, sitting among the polka-dotted pumpkins she'd sculpted—being surrounded by all of that beauty—being, by the patterns on her clothing, even made part of that beauty—but still wanting to destroy herself.

My impulse is the opposite. An impulse, not to destroy myself, but to create myself. To recreate myself. Again, and again, and again, and again, and again.